"I would have loved to help you make my bed. Or unmake it."

Even though her heart bumped hard, she gave him a chiding look. "Behave yourself. We said we were going to take this slowly, remember?"

"I know," he agreed a bit reluctantly. "Still, I can't help but fantasise occasionally."

Which of course made her heart pound harder at the thought of him fantasising about her. She moistened her lips, trying to think of something clever to say.

A low sound escaped him as the smile slid off his face. His gaze was on her mouth now, his eyes darkened to a deep emerald. His head dipped towards hers, though he paused just short of their lips touching. Giving in to her own desire, she closed the distance.

Available in April 2009
from Mills & Boon®
Special Edition

Finding Family
GINA WILKINS

MILLS & BOON
Pure reading pleasure™

First published in Great Britain 2009
by Harlequin Mills & Boon Limited,
Eton House, 18-24 Paradise Road, Richmond, Surrey TW9 1SR

ROM Pbk

ISBN: 978 0 263 87032 9

23-0409

Harlequin Mills & Boon policy is to use papers that are
natural, renewable and recyclable products and made from
wood grown in sustainable forests. The logging and
manufacturing processes conform to the legal environmental
regulations of the country of origin.

Printed and bound in Spain
by Litografía Rosés S.A., Barcelona

GINA WILKINS

is a bestselling and award-winning author who has written more than seventy books. She credits her successful career in romance to her long, happy marriage and her three "extraordinary" children.

A lifelong resident of central Arkansas, Ms Wilkins sold her first book in 1987 and has been writing full time since. She has appeared on the Waldenbooks, B Dalton and *USA TODAY* bestseller lists. She is a three-time recipient of the Maggie Award for Excellence, sponsored by Georgia Romance Writers, and has won several awards from the reviewers of *Romantic Times BOOKreviews.*

Prologue

The four-bedroom, two-and-a-half bath house was so empty that Mark Thomas's footsteps echoed when he walked through it. Gleaming wood floors were devoid of rugs, amplifying the sounds he made. Nothing hung on the walls.

Upstairs, a bed with no headboard and a small wooden chest were lost in the spacious master bedroom. One step down from the bedroom, a spacious dressing room led into a walk-in closet and an attached lounge with dormer windows that looked out over the front lawn. Except for his clothes, those areas were empty. The remaining three bedrooms were bare of furniture and decoration, though one held a half-dozen unpacked boxes filled with the few possessions he had brought with him to his new home.

Downstairs, a mismatched couch and chair had been placed haphazardly in the cozy front parlor, just to the left of the marble-floored foyer. The dining room on the opposite side of the entryway was empty. The ample, three-step-down end room that he thought of as a den, but which the Realtor had referred to as a gathering room, held only a large-screen television and a well-broken-in leather sofa.

In the kitchen, two wood-and-wrought iron bar stools provided the only seating. A small TV set, a coffeemaker and a microwave sat on the otherwise-empty U-shaped expanse of quartz countertops. The sunny breakfast room on the other side of the bar was as barren as the rest of his home.

He had owned the house for three weeks, and had lived in it for two. He had big plans for decorating, transforming the place from an empty shell to a warm, inviting home, which couldn't happen soon enough, as far as he was concerned. But for now, he found satisfaction in the awareness that for the first time in his thirty-two years, he was living in a home that was not a rental.

Besides, he reminded himself, the longer he took to get the decorating finished, the more time he would be able to spend with the pretty and intriguing designer he'd hired.

It was still early on this warm summer evening, not yet dark outside. Mark flipped on the overhead lights in the kitchen and opened the refrigerator door. He wasn't particularly hungry, but he rather liked the idea of preparing his own dinner in his own kitchen. Unfortunately, he thought as he closed the fridge door, it took more than a carton of orange juice, a quart of milk and a couple of individual-sized yogurts to make a meal.

Looked as though he would have to resort to delivery. Again. He was simply going to have to find the time to go to the grocery store soon. He moved toward the phone to call the closest Chinese delivery. He knew the number by memory.

The doorbell rang just as he punched in the second digit.

"Wow," he murmured, holding the receiver away from his ear and looking at it. "That was fast."

Chuckling at his own bad joke, he hung up the phone and walked through the echoing hallway toward the front door.

He didn't know the couple standing on the small covered porch. The dark-haired, dark-eyed woman was strikingly beautiful. The man had brown hair and eyes and a face that looked vaguely familiar, but not immediately recognizable.

"May I help you?" he asked, looking from the man to the woman and then back again.

The man spoke first. "Dr. Mark Thomas?"

"Yes."

"I'm Ethan Brannon. This is Aislinn Flaherty."

Neither name meant anything to him. "Nice to meet you." He added a slight upward note to the courtesy, an implied question.

Ethan looked at Aislinn, who nodded slightly, as if to encourage him. Mark waited patiently until Ethan turned back to him to say, "This is going to sound strange, I know, but I hope you'll give us the opportunity to explain. There's a, um—there's a chance that you and I could be brothers."

Brothers?

Mark felt the word slam into him, though he hoped he was able to hide the reaction as he stared at the couple. More specifically, at the man who looked vaguely familiar. Suspiciously like the man he saw in the mirror when he shaved every morning.

He opened the door wider and took a step backward. "I think you'd better come inside."

Chapter One

Rachel Madison's cell phone rang just as she parked her small SUV in the driveway of Mark Thomas's house in an upscale neighborhood outside Atlanta, Georgia. She glanced at the caller ID screen without enthusiasm. She wouldn't mind so much if the call were about business, but she doubted that she would be that lucky.

Recognizing the incoming number, she knew that luck was not on her side this time. "Hi, Mother," she said, holding the little phone to her ear.

"Rachel, you absolutely have to talk to your sister. She won't listen to a word from me."

"I'll talk to her," Rachel promised without even bothering to ask what she was supposed to say. "But I'm just about to meet with a client, so this is going to have to wait until later, okay?"

"First let me tell you what she said."

"I'll call you after my meeting and you can tell me all about it. But I really have to focus on my client now."

Her mother sighed heavily. "All right. I suppose you should concentrate on your work. That's more important right now."

Even though her mother couldn't see her, Rachel resisted an impulse to roll her eyes. "You know I don't consider work more important than family. It's just that I have an appointment."

"I'll let you go, then. Call me when you're finished, okay?"

"I will."

Closing the phone with relief, Rachel groaned when it buzzed again before she could even open her car door. This call, too, was from a number she recognized. "Hi, sis. Look, I've got a meeting—"

Typically, Dani didn't give her a chance to finish the sentence. "You have got to talk to Mother, Rach. She's gone too far this time. You have to tell her—"

"I'll talk to her," Rachel broke in rashly. "But I have to meet with a client, okay? He's expecting me right now."

"But—"

"I've got to go. I'll call you as soon as I'm free."

She hung up while her sister was still sputtering. Setting her cell phone to vibrate rather than ring, so that it wouldn't interrupt her meeting if it buzzed again—which it undoubtedly would—she reached into the backseat for the samples and drawings she had brought with her.

She always looked forward to presenting her ideas to her clients, but she had to admit that this meeting was especially exciting. Dr. Mark Thomas wasn't just any client. He was special. Attractive. Amusing. Intelligent. And the first client who had ever convinced her to mix business with pleasure and go out with him for an evening that had nothing to do with decorating.

It had been the most successful date she'd had in—well, in longer than she wanted to admit. No awkwardness, no stilted conversation, no discreet checking of watches, just a few hours of pleasant companionship. With a healthy dose of mutual attraction mixed in.

He'd been a perfect gentleman, leaving her at her door with a light kiss and an assurance that he would like to repeat the experience soon. She had gone to sleep that night replaying that brief, tantalizing kiss and fantasizing about a possible time when an evening together wouldn't end on her doorstep.

The outside of his house was quite nice, if a bit cookie-cutter, she mused, juggling her load on the walkway to his front door. A redbrick Georgian, its two-story center section was balanced by one-and-a-half story wings on either side. Each wing sported two white-fronted dormer windows. Three brick chimneys jutted up from the shingled roof, one on either side of the central section, the other at the end of the left wing.

Multipaned windows were arranged with perfect symmetry on either side of the house. In typical Georgian fashion, the paneled front door was centered in the middle section, the front porch covered by a triangular portico supported by four white pilasters. Four brick steps led up the porch. A row of shining, leaded-glass panes served as a transom above the white door, spilling more light into the foyer.

It wasn't a particularly large house by modern standards, topping out at just over four thousand square feet, but like the other similar size and style houses in the neighborhood, it proclaimed its owner as a successful young professional. Because she knew he had recently been made a partner in a thriving family-practice clinic, she doubted that Mark would have any trouble paying her fee.

Pausing at the door to shift the items she was holding and press the doorbell, she took a moment to reflect on how refreshingly well-adjusted Mark seemed to be. Educated, gainfully employed, apparently happy with his life, despite his lack of family. Perhaps happy *because* of that fact, she added wryly, though she didn't really believe that.

Such a welcome change from the string of users and losers that had made up her dating pool for the past three years, ever since her divorce from a needy, neurotic man who still hadn't completely accepted that she was no longer available to solve all his problems for him. She supposed she couldn't blame her ex for thinking of her in that light. Everyone else in her life certainly did, she thought with a glare down at her cell phone.

The door opened in response to her buzz. Mark stood in the doorway, blinking at her with an uncharacteristic frown.

She saw immediately that something wasn't quite right. He looked…disheveled, she decided. His typically neat brown hair was rumpled and there were shadows beneath his usually smiling green eyes. His old T-shirt and jeans had seen better days, a striking contrast to the impeccable, professional-casual clothing he had worn for their other meetings.

Judging from his expression, she would be willing to bet that he'd forgotten about this appointment. Which wasn't at all like the Mark Thomas she had come to know in the few weeks since she had first met him.

"Rachel," he said, almost as if it had taken him a moment to recognize her. "What…oh, damn. We had a meeting today."

So he *had* forgotten. She shifted the portfolio beneath her arm. "If this is a bad time, we can always reschedule."

"No. No, come in. I…" He pushed a hand through his hair, then shook his head impatiently. "I'm sorry. I'm afraid I'm a little distracted today."

She wasn't going to ask. Something had obviously happened to disturb him, but whatever it was, it was none of her business. Despite their one dinner date, he was a client, and she had no intention of getting involved in his problems. The very last thing she needed in her life was someone else's troubles, she assured herself firmly.

He closed the front door behind her and motioned her toward the nearly empty gathering room. "I had some news yesterday that's left me pretty shaken," he admitted. "I'm afraid I forgot about our meeting."

She absolutely was not going to ask. She paused at the top of the three steps that led down into the room. "We can always meet another time. Why don't you call me when you're ready to reschedule?"

"No, this is as good a time as any. Actually, I could use the distraction," he admitted, ushering her down into the room. "Can I get you anything to drink before we start? I have sodas or I could make some coffee."

"A glass of water sounds good." She wasn't really thirsty, but she thought fetching the water would give him a chance to pull himself together a bit, mentally prepare himself for the meeting that had slipped his mind.

"Okay. Make yourself comfortable, and I'll be right back." And then he looked around the sparsely furnished room and gave her a faint, wry smile. "Well, as comfortable as you can get, anyway."

"That's why I'm here," she reminded him brightly. "To help make your home comfortable for you and your visitors."

Still looking distracted, he nodded and headed for the kitchen.

Rachel spent the brief time alone setting up her portable easel, arranging the samples she had brought on the floor and opening her portfolio, all the while lecturing herself about how important it was for her to keep this meeting on a professional basis.

This was business, she reminded herself. For today, she was the hired decorator and Mark was her boss and client. The budding friendship—with potential for more—that had been developing between them was on hold for the afternoon. Maybe indefinitely, depending on how the next hour or so proceeded. All she wanted now was to put this meeting behind them so she could get to work and he could deal with whatever had been troubling him when she'd arrived.

He'd said he received some disturbing news. Had someone he cared about passed away? Was he in some kind of trouble?

She'd heard that doctors were always worried about being sued by disgruntled patients. She hoped Mark wasn't having to deal with a nuisance lawsuit.

None of her concern if he was, she reminded herself again.

He had seemed so happy when they'd gone out to dinner last week. Excited about his new partnership in a family clinic where he would begin practicing after taking a couple weeks off to get settled in his home. Elated to have purchased his first house, and looking forward to having her decorate it to suit his tastes and needs. Maybe even intrigued by the chemistry that had sparked between them from the start, as she had been.

He'd told her he was pretty much on his own in life. Raised by a single mother who had died several years ago, he claimed to have no other surviving family, only a network of good friends for emotional support. Despite her frequent frustration with her own ever-present and often-demanding family, she had found it rather sad that Mark had none of his own.

As exasperated as she became with them, she dearly loved her mother, siblings, aunts, uncles and cousins. She knew she could go to them in times of trouble, though it was more often the other way around. For some reason, everyone seemed to turn to her whenever they needed anything—and somehow she usually figured out a way to help.

She had a real problem saying certain phrases. Like, "Sorry, I can't." Or, "Ask someone else this time." Or just plain, "No." After many years of self-examination, she had come to the conclusion that she'd been born with a "backbone deficiency."

Which was why she was not going to get involved this time, she vowed. As alone in the world as he might be, Mark was a successful young doctor with a bright future and enough charm to float a boat. He didn't need any help from her, except for decorating this lovely but empty home.

Mark returned with the glass of ice water. "Here you go. Can I get you anything else before we start?"

His smile was a bit forced, his tone artificially cheerful, but she didn't let on that he wasn't fooling her for a minute. "No, this is fine, thank you."

Playing the game, she took a sip of the water, then looked around for a place to set the glass. Since there weren't any tables in the sparsely furnished room, she set it on top of her portfolio. "If you'll have a seat on the couch, I'll show you the designs and samples I've brought along. If you're still sure you want to do this now," she added.

"Absolutely." He sat on the couch, folded his arms and looked at her easel with such intense concentration that she almost sighed.

He was trying so hard to pretend he had put his problems out of his mind and was interested only in decorating. Once again, she found herself tempted to ask what had happened to upset him so, but she swallowed the question with a firm self-reminder that it was none of her business.

She began her presentation with the same thorough professionalism she would have used with any client. Room by room, she showed him the drawings she had made, the fabric samples and photographs of the furnishings she had selected for his consideration. He watched intently, studying everything she showed him, nodding whenever she paused for breath, fingering the fabric samples she handed him.

He agreed with everything she suggested. He didn't ask one question. And because he had been eagerly involved in discussions about his decor ever since his first meeting with her, she suspected that he was barely hearing a word she said.

Don't ask, Rachel, she admonished herself fiercely. *Don't get involved.*

"So, you like the cranberry paint for the dining room walls?" she asked him, tapping a crimson paint chip.

He stared blankly at the square of colored cardboard. "Sure. Cranberry. Okay."

He was breaking her heart. It was something about the look in his eyes. The slight slump of his shoulders. Whatever news he had received the day before, it had obviously hit him very hard. And maybe, she thought with a pang in her overly sensitive heart, there was no one for him to turn to for support or advice. Since he didn't have any family.

"I know it's a strong color, but I—" She swallowed. *Don't do it, Rachel. Keep it about the job.* "I think you'll really—"

After several moments of silence, he seemed to realize that she had stopped talking. "I'm sorry, did I miss something?"

Oh, give up. Setting down the paint chip, she moved slowly to sit beside him on the worn leather couch. "Do you want to talk about it?"

"About the red paint?"

She shook her head, resignation in her voice when she said, "About whatever is bothering you. I've been told I'm a very good listener."

So much for staying uninvolved…

Rachel really was intriguing. Fresh-faced, Mark supposed some would call her. She looked younger than her thirty years, with her dimpled pink cheeks, flawless skin and clear gray-blue eyes. Average height, slender physique, light brown hair she tended to wear in an attractively messy low ponytail. Not beautiful, exactly. But darned close.

And speaking of close…

Mark glanced down at the hand Rachel had rested on his knee as she sat only inches away from him on the couch. This was most definitely not a come-on. Without unwarranted conceit, he acknowledged that as a single, young doctor, he'd been at the receiving end of enough insincere gambits to know when someone was pretending to be interested in his problems.

Rachel was different. No hidden agendas here. No self-serving angles. She was the real thing. Or at least, that was the impression he'd gotten of her. He would hate to find out that he was wrong. It actually surprised him a bit to realize how very much he would hate that.

He should politely shrug off her question. Assure her that her concern was appreciated but unjustified. After all, this was a woman he had hoped to impress. Wanted to get closer to. It would hardly help his cause for her to find out what a mess his life had just become.

"Thanks, but I'm okay," he assured her. "Tell me more about this red dining room."

She shook her head. "I don't think you should be making decisions when you're this distracted. You could be surprised to find yourself living in a house you absolutely hate."

"I don't think that will happen. I trust your taste. That's why I hired you."

She smiled. "I appreciate that. But you made it clear that this project is very personal for you. You said you wanted input at every stage, and I want to make sure you have that. So we're not going to make any final decisions today. I'll leave everything with you to go through when you can concentrate. And in the meantime, if there's anything at all I can do for you—as a friend—I hope you won't hesitate to ask."

She really was a nice person, he thought, focusing on her sympathetic smile. Maybe she would understand if he told her about what had happened to him yesterday. As for her offer that he should let her know if there was anything she could do for him…

A glimmer of an idea formed in his mind.

"I had an unexpected visitor here yesterday," he began slowly. "Two of them, actually. A man and a woman. I'd never met either of them before."

Proving her assertion that she was a good listener, she merely nodded and waited for him to go on, her gaze focused on his face.

"The woman's name is Aislinn Flaherty. She claims to be a

psychic." Before this statement could fully sink in, he cleared his throat and added, "The guy's name is Ethan Brannon. And he says he's my older brother."

"Your brother?" she repeated in surprise. "You were raised as an only child, weren't you?"

He nodded grimly. Being told that he had a brother was actually the least jarring of the news he'd been given during that encounter. "My, um, my mother told me that my father died while she was pregnant with me. She said she had no family of her own and that his family didn't want anything to do with her or with me. We were on our own during my entire childhood, living pretty much hand to mouth, but generally happy."

"This man, Ethan Brannon—do you believe what he said? Is there a possibility that he is your brother?"

"More than a possibility. He pretty much convinced me. As convinced as I can be before we get the results of DNA testing, anyway."

"You're going to be tested?"

"We both are. Ethan insisted, and I agreed."

"So he claims he's your half brother? The result of a relationship your father had before you were born?"

"It's a little more complicated than that."

Her left eyebrow rose just a little. "Oh?"

"Ethan doesn't claim to be a half brother. He says he's my full brother—one of two, actually."

Rachel looked understandably confused. "There are two of them? And Ethan said you have the same parents?"

"Yes." He swallowed. "According to Ethan, my mother—er, the woman who raised me…"

Stopping abruptly, he shook his head. "Never mind. You don't want to hear this. I think we should talk about decorating. What did you say you want to do in here? Add tables, I hope."

"Definitely tables. But you were going to tell me what Ethan said about your mother."

He sighed. Might as well get this over with, he thought.

Rachel was bound to find out the truth if they became involved in a personal relationship, as he'd hoped.

"According to what Ethan told me, the woman who raised me kidnapped me from a loving family. Parents, and two older brothers. My—the woman I knew as my mother was the nanny. Thirty years ago, when I was barely two, she pushed her car into a flooded river and took off with me, leaving everyone to believe I was dead."

Rachel looked as though she wasn't sure she had heard him correctly. "Your mother…?"

He nodded grimly. "Wasn't my mother, after all. According to Ethan Brannon, my real mother is very much alive and living in Alabama with my father, an orthodontist. They are still unaware that their youngest son didn't drown as a toddler."

Chapter Two

Rachel had heard stories like this on television talk shows and in newspaper feature stories. She had never dreamed something so bizarre could happen to someone she actually knew. "This is…hard to believe. Did he have any proof?"

"His story was verified by one of my former patients last night. Posthumously."

The tale was growing more convoluted by the moment. "Post-humously? I don't understand. How—?"

Pushing a hand through his already disheveled hair, Mark grimaced. "Trust me, I know how strange it sounds. I'll try to tell you from the beginning—at least as much as I've figured out, myself."

Taking a deep breath, he began, describing a young married couple and their three boys who lived happily in North Carolina. The father was an orthodontist, the mother a housewife and active community volunteer, and because of their busy schedule, they hired a nanny to help them with their children, particularly the youngest son, Kyle.

The nanny, Carmen Thomas, became a part of the family, bonding closely with the children, especially Kyle. Explaining that she was alone in the world, she had seemed to find a purpose in her job and had been highly valued by her employers.

And then one day when Kyle was two, Carmen took the little boy out in a terrible storm. Flash flooding in the area had already claimed two lives, and no one knew why she'd left the house that day. Her car was discovered later, upside down in a flooded ravine. Though no bodies were found with the crushed vehicle, it was assumed that both the nanny and the child had been swept away, their remains buried beneath debris.

"Those poor parents," Rachel murmured, imagining how devastating it must have been for the Brannons to lose their youngest child.

Mark didn't seem ready to focus on emotions just yet. He was still struggling to deal with the facts of his past. "Unbeknownst to the Brannons, Carmen must have been planning the abduction for some time. The flooding proved to be a convenient cover for her disappearance. An acquaintance met her at the side of a mountain road that afternoon and helped her push her car into the water. The acquaintance then drove Carmen and the child out of the state."

"An 'acquaintance' helped Carmen kidnap a toddler?" Rachel shook her head in shocked disbelief. "No matter how close they were, what kind of a person would do that?"

"A person with serious emotional problems of her own. A woman who was told that she was rescuing a mother and her child from a violent domestic situation. During the ensuing few days, she began to suspect that she had been duped, but by then she felt that it was too late to change her course. She left the woman and child in Georgia and went on her way, trying to put them out of her mind. As I said, she had problems of her own."

"That still doesn't excuse what she did."

"No. And it haunted her for years, despite her efforts to forget. Years later, fate or…something brought her back into my life several months ago. She was the nursing home patient I told you about. She died yesterday, leaving behind a letter describing the role she had played in my abduction."

Growing more confused by the moment, Rachel shook her head. "Wait. How did she track you down? How did she know it was you? How did she become your patient in the nursing home?"

"Some of those questions I can't answer. The rest aren't really important right now. The fact is, I think I believe what she said. I think I am—or was—Kyle Brannon. Though I want the DNA tests to prove it, there's just something about it all that feels, well, true."

Maybe she was just naturally more skeptical than he. After all, she had a history of rescuing people from messes they'd gotten into as a result of being too gullible. Not that she thought of Mark as gullible, exactly, but still…

"If I were you, I would be very careful until after the DNA results become available. You said yourself that your former patient had emotional problems. The fact that Aislinn Flaherty claims to be psychic makes me very nervous. And you don't know this guy who suddenly appeared on your doorstep, claiming to be your brother. For all you know, this could be some sort of elaborate scam."

His lips twitched in a pitiful excuse for a smile. "Trust me, Rachel, I'm not quite as naive as you seem to fear. I'll insist on the DNA tests, and I won't do anything until after I've seen the results."

She studied his face, trying to read beyond the wry expression. "How do you feel about all this?"

After a rather lengthy pause, he cleared his throat. "I don't know, exactly. I'm having trouble processing everything."

She nodded, completely understanding why he would feel that way. All-too-familiar words left her mouth then, her typical, knee-jerk reaction to seeing anyone in distress. "Is there anything I can do for you?"

She couldn't imagine anything she could do, of course. This was so far beyond her realm of experience. And it wasn't as if she knew Mark particularly well, herself.

"Actually, there is something…"

She tried to hide her surprise. "Um, sure. What is it?"

"Join me for dinner tonight?"

"You want me to have dinner with you?" She couldn't see how another dinner date would help him with his family problem.

He nodded. "I'm supposed to meet Ethan and his girlfriend for dinner tonight. We all agreed it would be best to get together after I'd had a few hours to think about what they'd told me. It would be a really big help to me if you'd go with me tonight— you know, sort of moral support."

She cleared her throat. "I don't know, Mark. That sounds rather awkward."

"It would be even more awkward for me to have dinner with Ethan Brannon and his girlfriend without having anyone there who's on my side."

"Your side? You make it sound like a confrontation rather than a getting-to-know-each-other evening."

"I'm not expecting a confrontation. I just…well, I'd like to have someone there who knows me as Mark Thomas, you know? Not some missing kid named Kyle Brannon."

"You have plenty of friends you could ask. People who have known you much longer than I have."

"True. But you're the only one I've told," he replied with a disarming smile. "And I wanted to ask you out again, anyway. I was hoping to do so sometime during our meeting today—though, admittedly, I didn't have anything like this in mind at the time."

Nor had she envisioned that their second date would involve her going along as a buffer between him and his newfound brother.

Definitely an awkward situation, and she wasn't sure she wanted to get involved. She searched for the words to politely decline.

Before she could speak, her telephone vibrated against her waist. She glanced at the screen, grimacing when she saw that her sister was calling again. It seemed that she had a choice of how to spend her evening—either entertaining Mark's brother or refereeing yet another of her own family squabbles.

"Okay," she said abruptly, pushing her phone back into its holder. "What time?"

"That's a yes?" He seemed rather surprised that she had accepted, as if he'd realized how close she had come to declining.

She nodded. "Sure. Why not?"

His smile was wry. "I'm sure there are plenty of reasons why you'd have liked to pass, but I'm not going to argue. I'll pick you up at seven, okay?"

She nodded even as she ignored the renewed vibration of the phone at her waist. "I'll be ready."

At least as ready as she could be, she added silently.

"C'mon, Rach, you've got to help me out. I don't know how I'll get through the evening without you."

Holding her phone to her ear with one hand while she unzipped her slacks with the other, Rachel wondered absently when Robbie's voice had taken on this rather shrill, whining tone. She was sure he hadn't sounded that way when they had dated back in college. And it hadn't been quite this bad before their three-year marriage had broken up, though it had certainly become more common as their relationship had slowly dissolved.

"I'm sorry, Robbie. I told you, I have plans for tonight. I can't change them now."

"But what will I do? Kaylee just doesn't feel like working tonight. I can't have an empty hostess stand."

"Then you'll have to find someone else to fill in, because I can't do it tonight."

Robbie wasn't used to having Rachel stand her ground when he begged. Usually he could count on her to cave if he laid it on thickly enough. But not tonight, she vowed. She was already doing a favor for Mark. This time Robbie was going to have to find his own solutions to his problems.

"You're doing this to punish me, aren't you? Because I forgot to call you on your birthday last week. I know it hurt you that I didn't remember, but I've been overwhelmed with everything that's going on here. And Kaylee hasn't been much help—even though I guess she really does feel lousy, having a cold and all—but I've apologized to you over and over, Rachel. I don't know what else I can do."

Rachel sighed loudly as her clothing fell to the floor at her feet. "I'm not mad at you for missing my birthday. I just can't help you out tonight. I have other plans. You're going to have to find someone else. Mary can handle hostess responsibilities tonight. You'll have to call in one of the day staff to take up her serving duties. Call Hilary. She'll do it, if you pay her overtime. She needs the extra money."

"Mary's too impatient to be a good hostess. She doesn't have enough tact."

"She'll get better with practice. Or you're going to have to hire someone else if Kaylee continues to bail on you. The point is, you can't keep depending on me to come to your aid, Robbie. I have my own career. My own life."

"The restaurant was your dream, too, at one time," he reminded her, sounding more sullen than whiny now.

"It was never my dream. It was always yours. But I tried to support you in it—until you found someone else to be your cheerleader."

"So that's what this is about? You're still jealous about Kaylee?"

She nearly tripped over her fallen clothing. "Are you kidding me? I will always be eternally grateful to Kaylee. If you hadn't dumped me for her I might have spent years trying to hold our marriage together out of some misguided sense of loyalty and responsibility. This isn't 'about' anything, Robbie. I just can't help you tonight. I have a date, and I'm going to be late if I don't hurry. I'm hanging up now. I suggest you get on the phone to Mary and Hilary while you still have time to prepare for the dinner rush."

"A date? You didn't say you have a date. Who is the guy? Can't you reschedule for another—"

"Goodbye, Robbie." She snapped her phone closed and headed for the shower.

Mark didn't know why he was so nervous as he parked in the lot of Rachel's apartment complex. It was just dinner, right? A double date of sorts, over a nice meal. He'd been on dozens of outings like that. No big deal.

Of course, this would be the first time he'd dined with a man who claimed to be his brother. And the guy's sort-of psychic girl-friend. Not to mention a woman Mark, himself, had hoped to woo into his bed—once she'd selected a bed for him.

Wondering which of those factors made him most uneasy, he tugged at the collar of his deep blue shirt as he strode down the hallway of Rachel's apartment complex. He hadn't been sure what to wear. The restaurant where he and Ethan had agreed to meet wasn't a jacket and tie sort of place. He'd settled on a blue dress shirt, open at the collar, worn with khakis and brown oxfords.

And because he so rarely obsessed about his clothing, that was just another sign of how rattled he was this evening.

Rachel opened her door with a smile that made him forget any qualms he'd had about inviting her.

"You look great," he said.

"Thank you. I forgot to ask where we were going, so I wasn't sure what was appropriate to wear."

Only then did he notice what she had on, a sleeveless black dress with a knee-length hem. A small diamond pendant lay nestled in the tasteful amount of cleavage revealed by the V-neckline of the dress. Just enough of a glimpse to make him fantasize about seeing more.

"You look…great," he said again, unable to think coherently enough to come up with a new compliment.

Shallow dimples appeared in her cheeks, then quickly disappeared. Captivated by them, he simply stared at her until she cleared her throat and said, "Um, would you like to come in?"

Chiding himself for his uncharacteristic awkwardness, he shook his head—both to clear his mind and as a negative to her invitation. "We'd better go, if you're ready. Traffic's pretty heavy this evening."

"Just let me get my purse."

She returned after only moments with a small black bag tucked beneath her arm. Locking her door behind her, she smiled up at him, and only then did he see the slight hint of nerves in her eyes. "I'm ready."

It made him feel somewhat better to know that he wasn't the only one with hesitations about this outing. "Yeah. Me, too. And thanks again for going with me tonight, Rachel."

"Actually, you're helping me out, too," she confided, falling into step beside him.

"Yeah? In what way?"

"My mother and sister are squabbling and they're trying to put me squarely in the middle. I'd have had to spend the evening refereeing a family confrontation. I'd much rather deal with your family problems than my own tonight."

He laughed, as she had obviously intended for him to do. "Caught between a rock and a hard place, huh?"

She smiled up at him as he opened the passenger door of his car for her. "Not quite. You said you were planning to ask me out again today even before your brother showed up last night? I have to admit that I was hoping you would."

Pleased, he held the door while she slid into the seat. All of a sudden, he wasn't nearly as uneasy about the upcoming evening.

* * *

Rachel was struck immediately by the resemblances between Mark and Ethan Brannon. In his late thirties, Ethan was more sternly carved than Mark, with a few more lines around his dark green eyes and his mouth. And yet the similarities were so strong that most people would probably assume at first glance that they were related.

Their coloring, their build, something about the way they moved and spoke…within minutes she became convinced that the DNA tests would confirm Ethan's assertion. While she supposed it was possible that the resemblances were coincidental, it was highly unlikely.

As for Ethan's companion, Rachel thought Aislinn Flaherty was possibly one of the most beautiful women she had ever met. Perfect skin, gleaming waves of dark hair, exotically shaped dark eyes. Though she was drawn to Aislinn's warm smile and friendly manner, she sensed a reserve in the other woman that went very deep. A protective wall, perhaps.

Mark had called Aislinn a psychic, though his tone had made it clear that he was skeptical of that term. Rachel agreed. She had never put much stake into any suggestions of extrasensory abilities, figuring that most people who made such claims had a mercenary reason for doing so. But even after a few minutes she could tell that there was something different about Aislinn.

Sitting at a quiet table with drinks and appetizers, Rachel, Mark and Aislinn chatted politely about the nice weather they'd had that day. Ethan didn't seem the type to engage in small talk, judging by Rachel's early impression of him. He sat quietly watching them, and she suspected that he was the kind of man who chose to stay on the sidelines of life, observing more than participating. She doubted that he missed much of what went on around him, though he probably kept most of his thoughts to himself.

In that respect, he was very different from Mark. Mark was a participator, someone who could be found at the very heart of most activities, the middle of any crowd. From what she had gathered during their short acquaintance, small talk came easily to Mark, usually, though he seemed to be struggling a bit with Ethan. Mark was a people person, gregarious and concerned, both of which served him well in his job as a physician. Ethan, she learned, was a self-employed small-business consultant who worked out of his home in Alabama, spending more time with a computer than with his clients.

Ethan waited until the subject of the weather was exhausted before he joined the conversation, and then he jumped straight into a more serious topic. "I'm sure you've thought a great deal about everything you learned yesterday," he said to Mark.

"I haven't been able to think about anything else today," Mark admitted with a wry glance at Rachel. "As Rachel can attest. She and I were supposed to talk about furnishing my house today and I couldn't even concentrate long enough to pick paint colors."

"I'm a professional decorator," she explained when Ethan and Aislinn looked at her. She figured that was all they needed to know about her relationship with Mark at the moment.

Aislinn looked as though she would like to follow up on that tidbit, but Ethan stayed on topic. "I still haven't told the rest of the family that we found you. I knew you wanted time to think about everything first."

Looking a little nervous, Mark nodded. "I think we should wait until the DNA results come back before you break the news—just in case."

Ethan shrugged. "I don't have to wait. I know what the tests will show us."

"So confident," Mark muttered.

"I was old enough to remember when you disappeared. I remember what you looked like then—and I can see who you look like now. You look like a Brannon."

Rachel could almost hear Mark swallow hard in response to that blunt comment. She knew he was still trying to adjust to his new identity, that he didn't think of himself as a Brannon. She doubted that he knew how to think of himself at all now.

"That's not exactly indisputable evidence," he insisted. "We should wait until we have the test results."

"But that could take weeks."

"Ethan." Aislinn gave him a stern look. "Stop trying to railroad him. Give him time to come to terms with all of this."

"I gave him all day."

She snorted delicately. "One day to process having his entire life history changed? Seriously?"

"My history changed, too," he reminded her with a frown.

"Yes. But it's different for him. You've always known exactly who you are."

Mark cleared his throat. "I *am* still here."

Aislinn sent him a quick smile. "Sorry. We didn't mean to talk about you as if you weren't."

Rachel sighed when her cell phone rang in her purse. She'd forgotten to silence it again. At least she had the volume turned down low so that few people around would be bothered by the rings. Apologizing to her dinner companions, she fumbled in her purse, thinking that she would check the readout—just in case it really was important—and then mute the sound for the rest of the meal.

"It's your sister," Aislinn said. "I don't think it's an emergency."

"It's never a real emergency with Dani," Rachel replied in resignation. "Only in her own—"

She stopped abruptly as the significance of the number on her caller ID screen suddenly hit her. "How did you know it was my sister?"

Looking suddenly sheepish, Aislinn grimaced. "I'm sorry," she said again. "I guess I'm a little nervous, myself, tonight. I spoke without thinking."

Dropping the muted phone back into her purse, Rachel studied the other woman a bit warily. "Mark told me you're a psychic."

Aislinn winced. "I don't really like that word. I don't consider myself a psychic. I just get feelings sometimes that usually prove to be true."

"From what you told me, it's more than that," Mark interjected. "Ethan said you knew I was still alive after looking at a picture of me as a toddler, taken before I was…taken. You somehow sensed that I hadn't died in that flood, as my family believed."

Ethan nodded somberly. "It took her a while to convince me," he admitted. "I didn't know her very well when she first sprang it on me, and to put it bluntly, I thought she was trying to run some sort of scam on me. I probably wouldn't have even given her a chance to change my mind if she hadn't been my sister-in-law's longtime best friend. My sister-in-law's a cop—I figured she'd know if her best pal was a con artist."

"So you just thought I was crazy, instead," Aislinn said wryly.

Ethan gave her a look that was so blatantly intimate it made a funny little shiver run down Rachel's spine. Maybe it was a touch of envy, she decided, wondering what it would be like to have a man look at her quite that way.

"You managed to convince me otherwise," he murmured.

A slight touch of color tinged Aislinn's cheeks as she returned the look. There was no doubt in Rachel's mind that this couple was very much in love. It would have been interesting to watch that relationship develop, she mused, thinking of Ethan's initial skepticism of Aislinn's motives.

"You said your sister-in-law is a police officer?" she asked. "She's married to your other brother?"

Looking away from Aislinn, Ethan nodded. "Her name's Nic. She and Joel have only been married a couple of months."

"What does your brother do?"

With a faint smile, Ethan glanced at Mark. "He's a doctor. A pediatrician."

"It must run in the family," Rachel remarked, struck by the coincidence. "And you said your father is an orthodontist?"

He nodded. "And Mom's practically a professional community volunteer. The whole family is into taking care of other people. Which makes me the oddball."

"That's not true," Aislinn argued loyally. "You've helped dozens of small business owners in your consulting practice. Not being as social as the others doesn't make you an oddball."

"Who's the older brother?" Rachel asked. "You or Joel?"

"I'm the eldest. Joel's three years younger and Kyle, here's, a year younger than Joel."

Mark frowned. "I, uh, would rather you'd call me Mark. I know it wasn't the name I was given at birth—hell, it was given to me by the woman who stole me from my family—but it's the name I've used for thirty years."

"Sorry," Ethan said. "You have the right to answer to any name you like. The family will get used to thinking of you as Mark."

Looking somewhat grim, Mark reached for his water glass. "We've all got a lot to get used to."

Rachel rested her hand lightly on his knee beneath the table. It was a gesture of support and understanding rather than flirtation, and from the way Mark covered her hand with his own, she could tell that he accepted it that way. She could imagine how conflicted he must be about his eventual meeting with his parents and his other brother.

"It's going to be all right," Aislinn assured him kindly. "You have a very nice family. I'm sure you'll all develop a close friendship with time."

"Is that one of your psychic predictions?" Mark asked, sounding more prickly than Rachel had heard him before.

Though Ethan frowned in response to Mark's tone, Aislinn didn't seem to take offense. Perhaps she, too, understood the turmoil Mark must be experiencing. "It's just an educated guess. I've met all of your family, and I like them very much. As a matter of fact, I'm about to become a Brannon, myself. Ethan and I are going to be married."

Because Aislinn seemed to be making an effort to defuse

some of the tension at the table, Rachel cooperated eagerly. "That's wonderful news. How long have you been engaged?"

"About twenty hours," Ethan replied, glancing at his watch. "Not even long enough for me to buy her a ring yet."

Aislinn laughed softly. "I don't think she meant it quite so literally."

"Congratulations, you two." Mark was smiling again now. "That's great news."

"Thanks." Ethan looked amusingly proud. "We had a few rocky spots—mostly due to me, I'll admit—but she finally saw what a prize I am."

"And so modest," Aislinn added with a roll of her eyes.

Their food was delivered, and all of them concentrated for a few minutes on their meals, giving them a brief respite from trying to keep the conversation going. Ethan was the one who broke the silence, speaking to Mark with what Rachel was beginning to see as typical bluntness.

"I debated for a while about whether we should even try to find you. I knew you would have a life of your own, and I didn't know how you would feel about having a bunch of strangers suddenly claim to be your family. Aislinn convinced me it wouldn't be fair to any of us not to bring the truth to light. So—did we make the right call? Or do you wish we'd never shown up at your door?"

All eyes were on Mark as he considered his answer. Rachel suspected it was too early to ask that particular question. He didn't know yet *how* he felt about this dramatic turn his life had taken.

But then he sighed lightly and answered with equal candor. "I guess there's a part of me that wishes exactly that. Thirty-six hours ago, I knew exactly who I was and where my life was headed. Now—"

He shook his head. "Now everything is different. And I can't say I'm happy about that yet. But when it comes right down to it, I guess I wouldn't change your decision. I'd rather know the truth than to live the rest of my life in ignorance."

Ethan nodded, looking as though he both understood and approved of Mark's response. "I'd have felt the same way. You've got the option now of choosing how to proceed from here—but at least you have the facts."

"You're giving me the choice about whether to ever tell the rest of the family about me?"

Ethan hesitated—and then shook his head. "I'm afraid I can't do that. My, er, *our* parents have as much right to know the truth as you did. They may be strangers to you now, but you are their son, and they've spent thirty years grieving for you. They deserve to know the truth, even if it's going to be tough for them to hear."

Rachel couldn't imagine what it would be like for them. To suddenly discover that the baby boy they'd lost was now a grown man? That they had missed his entire childhood? That someone they had trusted had deliberately stolen those years from them?

She imagined that in some tiny way, it would be easier for them to believe he had died all those years ago, though primarily there would be joy that he had survived.

"I'm going to tell them," Ethan repeated. "But I'll consider your request to wait until after we get the DNA results. I can see your point about that giving us more verification of the story. Still, I don't like keeping it from them for that long."

"I think it would be best. If there's even the slightest chance that you're wrong, it would be cruel to tell them and then have to take it all back."

"I'm not wrong. But I'll wait—for a while. After that, it's up to you, I suppose, where we go from there. I hope you'll want to meet them, give them a chance to get to know you, but that's really your decision. I can't make you do anything."

"I'll meet them," Mark promised. "If the DNA comes back positive. But—"

"But you aren't exactly looking forward to it." Again, Ethan seemed to understand perfectly. "Can't say I blame you. I tend to go out of my way to avoid emotional encounters with other people."

Mark managed a smile. "Somehow that doesn't surprise me."

"You aren't the only one who's dreading telling the Brannons what really happened that day," Aislinn said, her expression grim now. "Ethan and I are going to announce our engagement—and then I'm going to have to tell them that it was my mother who helped Carmen kidnap you that afternoon."

Chapter Three

"Your mother?" Rachel blurted before she could stop herself. Aislinn grimaced. "I thought Mark had told you the whole story."

"He said Carmen had an accomplice—someone who had been told she was helping a woman take her child out of an abusive situation."

And then Rachel remembered what else Mark had told her about that woman. "He said she was his patient at the long-term care facility. And that she—"

"She died before Ethan and I arrived in Atlanta, leaving a letter telling the whole story," Aislinn finished evenly. "I can't begin to understand exactly how she ended up in Mark's care, though I think she somehow arranged that on her own. I don't know how it happened that my best friend married Mark's brother, bringing me into their lives and leading Ethan here. I can only assume that some higher power intervened to bring justice to a family that had suffered entirely too much."

"I'm very sorry about your loss."

"Thank you. But I didn't actually know her," Aislinn said with a rather sad little shrug. "She left me with my grandfather and my great-aunt when I was only six months old. My mother was a restless spirit with a lot of emotional baggage. She had special gifts of her own, but she never learned to live comfortably with them. She spent many years engaging in self-destructive behavior and making poor judgment calls, such as helping Carmen smuggle Mark out of North Carolina. She ended up dying alone in the nursing home, a wealthy widow with multiple sclerosis and a guilty conscience."

And Rachel had thought *her* family was complicated. "This is all very strange."

"Tell me about it," Mark muttered.

"Maybe we should spend some time getting to know each other," Aislinn suggested, apparently trying to lighten the mood for the remainder of the meal. "Mark, you said you're decorating your house?"

He nodded, taking advantage of the opportunity to change the subject. "I just moved in a couple of weeks ago and I didn't bring much with me from my old apartment. I hired Rachel to help me furnish and decorate, make the place look nice and comfortable."

"That sounds like fun."

"Not to Ethan," Rachel speculated, studying his expression.

Ethan gave her a wry smile. "I've got to admit decorating doesn't really interest me. I buy furniture that's comfortable and functional and I arrange it in a way that's most practical for me. Aislinn, now, likes that sort of thing. She's a professional cake designer."

Intrigued, Rachel asked Aislinn several questions about her business, and Aislinn responded in kind, so that they were soon talking like old friends. Rachel was even able to forget about Aislinn's "gifts" for a little while, and enjoyed visiting with a woman with whom she had quite a few things in common. Ethan and Mark listened, neither adding much to the conversation.

She didn't know how much help she had given Mark this

evening. She'd been more of an intrigued spectator than a supporter, despite their brief under-the-table bonding.

They were almost finished with their desserts when Aislinn glanced at Rachel's purse. "Your phone's ringing again."

Lifting her eyebrows, Rachel looked down at the purse. "But I turned off the ringer."

Ethan shook his head in resignation. "If she says it's ringing, you can bet it is."

Pulling out the phone, Rachel checked the screen. "You're right, it is. I don't suppose you can tell me who's calling?"

Hearing the hint of a challenge, Aislinn smiled faintly. "Not this time. I don't think it's an emergency, though."

"Not to me, it isn't." Knowing Robbie would disagree, for that was who was trying to reach her, probably with another woeful tale of how understaffed he was at his restaurant that evening, Rachel slipped the phone back into her purse. "Funny how it always seems to be an emergency to whoever's calling me."

Aislinn searched her face, and Rachel had the uncomfortable feeling that the other woman, whether psychic or simply intuitive, saw entirely too much. But all she said was, "Some people get so busy taking care of everyone else that they leave no time to see to their own needs."

Because that comment was all too applicable to her life, Rachel lifted her coffee cup to avoid having to respond.

Mark parked in the lot of Rachel's apartment complex and wondered even as he turned off the engine if this would be the last time he would drive her here. He was rethinking yet again his decision to ask her to accompany him. Considering how nervous and uncomfortable he had been all evening, not to mention the inherent awkwardness of the entire situation, it would be a surprise if she ever agreed to go out with him again.

Which would be a shame, he thought regretfully. He really liked her, wanted to see her again—and not just for business. But he couldn't blame her if she decided his life was in too much turmoil right now for her to get involved with him. Especially since she had confided that she had family problems of her own.

Without giving her a chance to decline, he opened his car door to walk her to her apartment. If this was to be their last date, he wanted to make it last a while longer.

"Would you like to come in for coffee?" she surprised him by asking when they reached the door.

He studied her expression to try to determine if she meant it or if she was only being polite. Because he wanted to accept, he decided it didn't matter why she'd asked. "Yeah, that sounds good."

He was curious how the decorator had done her own apartment. He liked what he saw—which boded well for his own place. He had seen pictures of her work, of course, but it was even better to see such a personal example. "Nice."

"Thank you. I know it's a little modern for your tastes, but it all seemed to work with the architecture here."

Studying the clean lines of her furniture and the bold, sleek shapes of the accessories she had chosen, he nodded. "I agree."

"Have a seat. I'll put the coffee on."

He settled on the couch, watching her leave the room. He really enjoyed watching her walk. Not too blatantly sexy, but just seductive enough to kick his libido up a notch.

Telling himself to rein it in, he looked around the room again. The basic theme was muted—midtoned woods, neutral fabrics, soft beige paint on the walls. Soothing and comfortable, with an occasional shock of bold, primary color to keep it from being too monotonous. A vivid red pillow. A cobalt-blue vase. A splash of bold green in a painting.

It was a lot easier to admire Rachel's decor than to dwell on his own tumultuous emotions.

She returned carrying two mugs of coffee. "Sorry I took so long. I needed to check my messages."

"It didn't feel like that long. You get a lot of calls, don't you?"

She made a wry face as she handed him his mug and settled on the couch beside him. "I'm afraid so. My family's in the habit of thinking of me as their own personal 'Dear Abby,' on call 24-7."

"So you're the family caretaker?" He looked at her over the rim of his mug as he took a sip of the excellent coffee. "Most families seem to have someone who serves in that capacity, from what I've observed. Not from my own experience, of course."

She shrugged. "I sort of fell into the role. My mother's a dear woman, but my father spoiled her a bit. Ever since he died a couple of years ago, she has expected me to continue that pattern. I'm the oldest, you see. My sister, Dani, is three years younger, and my brother, Clay, just turned nineteen. Dani and Clay always seem to be in some scrape or another."

"So you get to be the responsible one."

She smiled. "I don't really mind. Most of the time."

"Between running your business and taking care of your family, it must be difficult for you to find time for yourself."

She shrugged, which he supposed was an answer in itself. "I would think you'd have the same problem, considering your very demanding career."

"Yes, well, I'm taking a few weeks off before starting the new practice. And I don't have a family to worry about once I do start—er, at least I haven't to this point."

"You're having trouble dealing with all of this, aren't you?"

He set his mug on a coaster on her low coffee table. He was tired of talking about his newfound family. Besides, he didn't like thinking of himself as someone else who needed to unload his problems on Rachel's sympathetic shoulders. "I'll get used to it. Look, I'm sorry tonight was so weird and awkward. I hope it didn't scare you off from going out with me again—just the two of us next time."

She smiled faintly. "I didn't think tonight was so weird. I enjoyed meeting Ethan and Aislinn. They're both very interesting people. As for you—I don't scare that easily. If I did, I wouldn't have gone out with you in the first place. I usually have a firm rule about not dating clients, especially when a job is ongoing—or in our case, just barely started. Had I been worried about consequences, I would have made an excuse not to have dinner with you last week."

He found her straightforward manner very refreshing. If she was this candid in all her responses to people, it was no wonder so many came to her for advice and support.

He smiled. "I don't usually mix business with pleasure, myself. Asking you out during our second business meeting was hardly my style. But I just couldn't resist."

Dimples flashed in both her cheeks with her smile. "I rather like being irresistible."

He reached out to trace one of those alluring dimples with the pad of his right thumb. "You are."

A hint of pink warmed her cheeks, but it didn't seem to be caused by embarrassment. Rather, he thought he saw the same awareness in her eyes that he was feeling, himself. Which gave him the courage to lean his head closer to hers. The way she tilted her face upward was all the encouragement he needed to press his mouth to hers.

He had kissed her once before, briefly, when they had concluded their one previous dinner date. Just a tantalizing brush of lips that had left him hungry for more. This time he allowed himself to linger, and he was rewarded when she responded with an eagerness that mirrored his own. Maybe he hadn't been the only one hoping that one initial kiss would lead to more?

He slid his arms around her, and hers went around his neck. She felt so good against him. Slender, yet strong, rather than fragile. Cooperative rather than yielding. When her lips parted for him, it was as much demand as invitation.

No shy ingenue here, but a woman with the confidence born of experience. He wouldn't have wanted it any other way.

Her brown hair waved softly around his fingers when he

buried his hand at the back of her head. He loved the clean, natural feel of it. Her own fingers toyed with the shorter hair at his nape, causing a shiver of reaction to zip down his spine.

She tilted her head to a new angle, drawing in a quick breath before diving into the next kiss. He closed his eyes and went under with her, letting currents of sensation carry him away.

They were drifting downward toward the sofa cushions behind her when the telephone rang. Its shrill chime shattered the intimacy of the moment. As much as he wanted to pretend he didn't hear it, he felt a sudden tension grip Rachel, and he knew the interlude was over.

Just as well, he told himself, drawing reluctantly away. It was too soon for this, anyway. And the timing wasn't exactly ideal, considering everything else that was going on in his life right now.

Now if only he could believe any of that.

Her expression, which fell somewhere between regret and reprieve, told him that she was having a very similar internal dialogue. Sliding away from him, she reached for her phone and glanced at the caller ID screen. A sigh escaped her, and she set the phone down without bothering to answer. "I'll let voice mail take it."

"Don't miss a call on my account."

She shook her head. "It's my ex-husband. I'm not particularly interested in talking to him right now."

He knew she'd been married; she had mentioned it briefly during their first dinner together. He had not known that she stayed in contact with her ex.

The mood was most definitely broken. He pushed a hand through his hair and stood. "It's getting late. I'd better go. Thanks again for going with me tonight."

She walked him to the door. "So you and Ethan are going to have your tests Monday morning?"

He nodded. "They're heading back home after that. Apparently, he's led everyone to believe he's on a business trip."

"You still think it would be best for him not to mention you to the rest of the family until the test results are back?"

"Yeah. I still want him to wait."

"How long will it take?"

"A couple of weeks, most likely. If the lab's backed up, it could take three."

"That's a long time to ask him to keep such a big secret."

"It's been thirty years," he said with a shrug. "They can wait another few weeks."

She didn't look convinced, but she didn't argue with him. "Do you think you and Ethan will stay in contact while you wait for the results?"

He smiled slightly. "I won't hang up on him if he calls. I don't think Ethan's much of a phone chatter, though."

"No. Neither do I."

He reached for the door.

"You know what the test will say, Mark," she said quietly as his hand fell on the doorknob.

He paused without looking back at her. "I'm not psychic like Aislinn."

"You don't really have to be, do you?"

He sighed. "No. I'm pretty sure I'm exactly who Ethan said I am. I just need to see the test results before I make any decisions, you know?"

"You should do what feels right to you."

He wished he knew what that was. "I'd like to schedule another meeting with you about my house. I'll look at all the samples and drawings you left there and I'll try to be more informed and coherent next time we talk."

"I'm free for a while tomorrow afternoon. Or would you rather wait until—"

"Tomorrow sounds good," he said, jumping on the offer before she could change her mind. "What time?"

"What about Ethan and Aislinn? Don't you have any plans with them tomorrow?"

"Not really. I think they're going to do some sightseeing around Atlanta tomorrow. We're meeting for breakfast Monday morning before the DNA test."

She frowned a little, and he suspected he knew what she was thinking. She probably thought he should have offered to entertain the other couple in his town. To be honest, he felt a little guilty about not doing so. But the truth was, he just hadn't known what to do with them—not while he was still struggling to think of them as family. He was well aware that he was using the DNA test as a way to stall for a few more weeks before he had to fully face the looming changes in his life.

To his relief, she decided to follow his lead and concentrate on her work rather than his complex personal situation. "Two o'clock?"

"I'll be ready," he promised.

He was in a surprisingly good mood as he headed back to his car. It had nothing to do with his newfound family. Little to do with his renewed decorating plans. And everything to do with the fact that even after this not particularly spectacular evening, Rachel still seemed to be interested in him.

"Where have you been? I've been trying to call you all evening," Dani scolded her sister, less than half an hour after Mark left.

"That's why I called you back," Rachel answered with forced patience. "I couldn't talk earlier, but now I can. What do you want?"

"I need to talk to you. What have you been doing all day, anyway?"

"I spent the day with a client." She saw no need to go into any further detail.

"You work too hard, Ray-Ray. All day on a Saturday?"

There was no mistaking the genuine concern in Dani's voice, and Rachel softened in response. "Don't worry about me, sis. You know I enjoy my job."

She felt a little guilty for leading her sister to believe she'd been working all day, rather than sharing a strictly personal dinner with Mark, but she didn't give in to it. She wasn't anywhere near ready to confide in Dani that there could be a new man in Rachel's life. Dani would tell their mom, and then the two of them would hound Rachel for details and start offering unwanted advice.

"I know. But you should leave time for yourself, too."

It was eerily reminiscent of what Aislinn had said earlier. Rachel cleared her throat, her guilt intensifying. "Um, Dani—"

"Besides, I really needed to talk to you today. Mother's driving me nuts. You've got to help me convince her to get off my case about Kurt."

Guilt dissipated in a puff of exasperation. "This is really between you and Mother. I don't want to get in the middle this time."

"But you have to talk to her. She'll listen to you. She's never listened to me."

"Maybe because you get too defensive and argumentative with her. If you would just stay calm and discuss her concerns and then quietly present your own position, it would be so much more productive for both of you."

"She's the one who won't stay calm. She starts ragging on me about Kurt and then trying to tell me how to live my life, and then when I calmly tell her that I'm old enough to know what I'm doing and I don't really need her to make my decisions for me, she tries to make me feel guilty and irresponsible."

Amazing how oblivious Dani could be about her own behavior, Rachel thought with a shake of her head. Anyone who'd heard that aggrieved speech would think that she was completely innocent in her frequent disagreements with her mother. Rachel, who had been a spectator for all too many of those head-to-heads, knew better.

Dani was always the first to raise her voice, the first to burst into tears, the first to claim that no one cared about her or what she wanted. Clay hadn't dubbed Dani the drama princess for nothing. Their mother, he had added, was still the queen. When Dani asked what that made Rachel, he had merely shrugged and said Rachel was the "executive producer"—frantically putting out fires behind the scenes.

"And where do you fit into this scenario you've created?" Dani had asked pointedly.

With a shrug, Clay had replied, "Me? I'm just a member of the audience."

That response still bothered Rachel when she thought about it. Losing his father in his teens and being raised in a household of strong-willed and very vocal women had not been particularly easy for Clay. As a result, he had searched for his identity outside the home—and she wasn't thrilled about some of the places in which he had looked. Where he was still looking.

But she had to focus on her other sibling for now. "Dani, you can't blame Mother for being worried about you. Let's face it, you haven't always made the best choices when it comes to men. And Kurt *is* married."

"Don't you start, too," Dani said, immediately on the defensive. "He's getting a divorce."

"He's been saying that for months. There's been no evidence of it. Can't you admit that there is reason to be concerned that he's using you, Dani? That he has no intention of getting a divorce, but every hope of keeping you obligingly on the side for a while longer?"

"Now you sound just like Mother. I didn't call you for a lecture."

"No, you want me to argue your point to Mother. And I'm sorry, but I can't do that. I'll stay completely out of it, but I won't try to defend Kurt."

"Well, thanks a lot."

"There's no need to snap at me. I'm not going to side with her, either. I'm not getting involved either way."

"Neither one of you will listen to me. You're both being closed minded and judgmental. If you would just give Kurt a chance…"

Rachel had heard this spiel all too many times. She cut in firmly, "I'll listen to you anytime you need to talk, but I'm not arguing with Mother for you. Now, it's getting late, and I'm tired. So, good night. I'll see you soon, okay?"

"Fine. Great. Be that way. I won't bother you with my problems again."

She wished, Rachel thought as she closed her phone after Dani summarily ended the call. But she would bet that she hadn't heard the end of this argument.

Chapter Four

"Would you rather start in here," Rachel asked, walking into Mark's bedroom, "or downstairs? It's up to you."

Mark looked around the bare room, his gaze lingering on the unadorned bed covered with a set of plain beige sheets and a green blanket. "Wherever you prefer to begin. Either option works for me."

She followed his glance toward the bed, noted the head-shaped indention in the single pillow and, clearing her throat, turned quickly away. "Well, if you plan to entertain, you'll want the gathering room finished first for your guests. But some people want their own personal space done first, just so they'll have a beautiful room to wake up in."

She hoped it wasn't obvious to him that even as she spoke, she pictured him waking up in this room, all warm and tousled and heavy-eyed. The image made her mouth go dry.

She moistened her lips discreetly. "So, while I can have crews doing some work in more than one room at once, you'll need to decide which one you want to focus on, if you still want to be actively involved with the selection of furnishings and decorations."

Some clients were content to let her make all the choices, consulting with them very little during the process. Mark, on the other hand, had said he wanted to approve every item she brought in, though he was open to her suggestions. She didn't mind working either way, though she'd had clients who had driven her nuts with their indecisiveness or frequent mind changes. She thought working with Mark would be a pleasure—in many ways.

"It will be nice to have this room done." Standing beside the empty fireplace topped with a bare wood mantel, Mark looked around the large, spartanly furnished space with a wry smile. "Blank walls aren't exactly the first thing I want to see every morning. And that bed has never been particularly comfortable. I just never got around to replacing it while I lived in the apartment I rented before. Probably because I knew I wouldn't stay there long."

"We'll make sure you have a comfortable mattress. And that mahogany-framed bed with the paneled headboard we picked out is going to look great in here, especially when we add the double dresser and side tables. And a bench at the foot of the bed, so you can sit to put on your socks and shoes. With some nice artwork on the walls and a gorgeous rug to center the room, it will look amazing in here, I promise."

"I believe you," he said with a smile. He waved an arm toward the doorway that led down into the dressing room, closet and lounge. "We'll do those areas while we're at it, won't we? It'll be nice to have the lounge furnished for reading and watching TV in the evenings."

"Yes, of course, we'll work in there at the same time. The decor of the lounge will carry over from in here, making the rooms flow beautifully together. I want this suite to feel like a private retreat to you, a place to unwind and recharge."

"I like the sound of that."

She glanced again at the bed, and was aware that she was having to work to keep her attention focused on decorating. "So, this room and then the gathering room?"

"Sure. I don't plan to entertain anytime soon, anyway."

Not even his newly discovered family? Or was his lack of furniture and decoration another excuse for avoiding that meeting? She made a mental note to get as much done as possible at the same time in both his bedroom suite and the gathering room. He would have to meet his family eventually, and she thought he should have a nice place in which to entertain them.

Not that she was getting involved, she assured herself firmly. She was just doing her job.

"So, when are we going shopping?" Mark asked, rubbing his hands together in a gesture of anticipation. "I've got a few more days before I start my new practice. I'd like to have this project well underway before then."

She laughed. "We can start whenever you're ready. Except for a couple of minor details to take care of during the next few weeks, you're my primary client right now."

With what he'd agreed to pay her, she didn't really need another client at the moment, she thought in private satisfaction. The price they'd agreed upon was fair, but generous.

"So we can start tomorrow?"

"Aren't you getting the DNA test tomorrow?"

"Yeah, but I'll be finished by noon. We could meet somewhere at, say, one o'clock."

"You don't want to spend the rest of tomorrow with Ethan?"

"He's leaving town immediately after the test. He said he has to get back to work, and so does Aislinn."

It still bothered her a little that he wasn't trying to spend more time with his long-lost brother. It seemed to her that they would want to get to know each other better while they had this opportunity.

She suspected that Ethan considered himself to be giving Mark time and space, but that he would have been agreeable to seeing more of each other while he was in town. Mark was the one who was erecting barriers—both emotional and physical.

Still none of your business, Rachel, she told herself. "Okay, we can start tomorrow. We can meet at McClain's Home Furnishings at one."

"Great. Now, have we finished all our business for today?"

They had spent more than an hour discussing her drawings, samples and catalogs prior to coming upstairs to his bedroom to make a few final decisions. Unlike the last time they'd tried to consult, Mark had been fully engaged, asking lots of questions, vetoing a few ideas he didn't like at all, making some suggestions and enthusiastically welcoming hers.

"Yes, we've done pretty much all we can for today. The painters should be able to start by Wednesday, and in the meantime, we can shop. You'll have to order much of your furniture, so it will be a few weeks before it all comes in."

Mark wasn't the type who wanted to furnish his house at leisure, spending a long time shopping for just the right pieces for each room. He'd already informed her that he wanted the place completely furnished and decorated within a month, if possible, so that he would have a fully livable home in which to start his new medical partnership. She would almost call his behavior "nesting." Which her friend Kristy, a former psychology student, would be sure to interpret as a readiness to settle down, start a family, move into the next phase of his life.

She swallowed hard, and told herself it would be wiser not to pursue that line of thought much further.

She had told him before, of course, that decorating was not an overnight process, but he always seemed to hope she had overstated the time frame. "That long?"

"A few weeks is actually pretty quick for an entire house. Had you wanted any carpentry work or other major renovations, you'd have been looking at a minimum of three months."

"Then it's just as well I like the house as it is, isn't it? I can't think of anything I'd change other than the wall colors, which we've chosen."

"Yes, you were fortunate to have these beautiful wood floors. And the stone floor in the kitchen is exactly what I would have chosen for you, myself."

He nodded. "So, now that you're off the clock, so to speak, how about having dinner with me this evening? *Not* to talk about decorating."

"I would love to," she replied, "but I can't. I have to go to my mother's for dinner tonight."

He managed to look both disappointed and amused. "You sound so eager."

She wrinkled her nose in response to his ironic tone. "I know. I wish I could be more enthusiastic about it. I love my family, I really do—but when my mother and my sister start in on one another, as they undoubtedly will tonight, I want to lock them in separate rooms."

"Still feuding, huh?"

"Pretty much. Dani's seeing someone Mother doesn't approve of, and—" She suddenly stopped and shook her head, wondering what she was doing. She never talked about her personal life to her clients. Not that Mark was strictly a client, but still. "You wouldn't be interested."

"I'm interested in everything about you," he replied simply. "And, after all, you're learning all about my, er, family."

She'd even had dinner with a couple of them. And that thought sparked an idea. Something about turnabout being fair play. "Why don't you join us this evening?"

His eyebrows rose in surprise. "You're inviting me to dinner with your family?"

She gave herself a moment to reconsider. Taking him to dinner could cause problems in itself. And yet, her family was much less likely to bicker when they had company at the table. For one thing, they would be too interested in grilling him about everything from his family history to his intentions toward Rachel.

But she had already blurted out an invitation, and she wouldn't take it back now. "Yes, but feel free to beg off. I mean, I can understand if you'd rather not—"

"I'd love to."

"Um—you would?"

"Absolutely. I'd enjoy meeting them."

"I warn you, they can be a little nosy. So, be prepared. They'll probably want to know all about you. There's no need for you to tell them about your family history right now. I'm sure you would rather not talk about that with strangers."

"I don't even like to think about it myself, yet," he admitted, confirming her earlier speculations. "But I'm pretty good at politely evading interrogations when I want to. My geriatric patients don't even blink before asking the most personal questions you can imagine."

She chuckled. "I can imagine. My grandmother used to grill all my boyfriends mercilessly. One of them told me it was like being in a confessional with his priest. Another likened it to being interrogated by a homicide detective."

"Guess I'm lucky I missed that."

She grinned. "What makes you think that? Grandma is still very much alive, and she'll be at dinner tonight."

He laughed, and she loved the sound. It was nice to know that she'd taken his mind off his own family problems for a little while. "So, how are you going to introduce me?"

"I'll just refer to you as a new client," she promised.

"Are you in the habit of bringing clients home to dinner?"

"No. You'll be the first, actually."

She wasn't sure when he had moved closer. She didn't remember seeing him take any steps. "That makes me feel very special," he murmured.

Something about his smile made a delicious shiver run down

her spine. "I would tell you that you are, but that might give you a big head."

He lifted a hand to run his fingertips along her jawline. "I think you're pretty special, too."

Suddenly very much aware that they were standing in his bedroom, she cleared her throat. "Why don't I pick *you* up this time? Around six-thirty?"

"Sounds good," he murmured. "And while we're still on personal time…"

He lowered his head to press his mouth to hers.

"The hydrangeas really are beautiful, aren't they?" Aislinn mused, gazing at a rather spectacular display of bright purple blooms. "I love it here in the shade garden. It's so much cooler under these big trees."

"Yeah. It's nice."

She looked up at Ethan with a chiding expression. "You're drifting again. You aren't even seeing these beautiful flowers."

He gave a shrug that was only partially apologetic. "I didn't come to Atlanta to visit the botanical gardens."

"I know. But you knew I wanted to see them. The same reason you spent two hours in the High Museum of Art before we came here."

His expression softened. "Have you had a good time?"

Leaning against his arm, she smiled up at him. "I've had a wonderful time. And I can't wait to visit the aquarium when we leave here. These are the three places I've always wanted to see in Atlanta."

"Then I'm glad we had the chance to do so. Tonight I'll take you somewhere special for dinner, if you like. I know a couple of really good Atlanta restaurants where I've eaten on business trips to the area."

"That sounds wonderful. It's been a lovely day, Ethan. A very special way to celebrate our engagement."

"So I guess it's a good thing that Mark blew us off today?" he muttered.

"He didn't blow us off. He just needs time. You, of all people, should understand. Didn't you need time to adjust to the changes in your life after you met me? Isn't that why you barricaded yourself alone in your river cabin for a couple of weeks while I stewed about whether you would ever let me get close to you again?"

"Well…yeah, I guess. But that was different."

"How?"

"You had told me something that was very difficult to believe, with little evidence to back you up. And I wasn't sure I was ready to get involved with someone who would always know what I was thinking and feeling."

"Not always," she murmured with a rueful little smile. "But this isn't about us. You've told Mark something that's hard to believe, and you've offered little evidence to back up your story. If what you've said is true, everything he's always believed about his family history, about his very identity, down to the name on his birth certificate, is wrong. Based on lies told by someone he loved and trusted. You can't expect him to just accept all of that without going through some private turmoil."

"Well, no, I guess not. But I can't get a read on him, Aislinn. I can't tell what he's thinking, how he feels about any of this. Maybe you can?"

"I know he's confused. And anxious. He knows what you've told him is true, but he isn't allowing himself to think about it too much yet. He seems to be focusing on other things to distract himself from having to deal with the reality of what he has learned this weekend."

"Focusing on what other things?"

"His house, I would guess. And Rachel. He seems very taken with her."

"He's got a lot going on now. New family, new job, new house, new girlfriend. I can see why he's been feeling some stress," Ethan conceded.

Frowning, Aislinn nodded slowly. "Yes. It's a lot for anyone to have to deal with. And it's going to be tough for him. I just hope everything works out for him."

"You don't know?"

"I know he's facing a hard decision. Whether it's with the family or Rachel, or something else altogether, I don't know. Nor can I predict how it will all turn out for him. That's all I've got."

Reaching down to take her hand, Ethan began to stroll down the shady path again. "Funny how this gift of yours works. You seem to have little control over it, actually."

"I have almost no control over it. I wish I could just concentrate somehow and have all the answers—but it doesn't work that way. All I can do is explain it to you the way I always have—I get flashes of insight. Strong hunches, some might call them. I don't do anything in particular to cause them, and I don't always know what they mean, or how to interpret the sketchy information I get. You can't just ask me questions and get the answers as if I were some sort of Magic 8-ball toy."

Laughing, Ethan held up his free hand. "Okay, I get the picture. You'll have to forgive me if I'm still getting used to all of this. It's only been a few days since you completely convinced me that you really do have a gift."

"I'm not offended," she assured him. "I just want you to understand what you're getting into with me."

He looked down at her with a rare, full grin. "I know exactly what I'm getting into. And I consider myself a lucky man for it."

Pleased, she moved a little closer to his side.

Rachel stopped her SUV in front of her mother's house, put the gear shift into Park, and then seriously considered throwing it into Reverse and driving away again. What had she been thinking to bring Mark with her to a family dinner? Sure, she had gone to a sort-of family dinner with him, but that was different. Those were much more normal people—a newfound older brother and his psychic girlfriend. Compared to *her* family, just run-of-the-mill.

Sitting in the passenger seat, Mark laughed. "For some reason, I find myself thinking of the time I drove my friend J.T. when he had outpatient hernia surgery. His expression before we went into the clinic looked very much like yours does now. Are you really dreading this evening so much?"

She wrinkled her nose. "It's not as bad as hernia surgery. I just hope you don't regret coming with me."

"I'm looking forward to meeting your family."

She had tried to warn him about them on the way over, but no one could really be prepared for her family without actually meeting them. "Okay," she said, reaching for her door handle, "let's get this over with."

He was laughing again when he slid out of his seat.

Her mother's blue-shuttered, white frame house was straight out of a country cottage decorating magazine. Two wicker rockers sat on the front porch beneath a ceiling fan. A wicker table between them held a big pot of multicolored gerbera daisies. A large ceramic cat sat by the front door, next to a mat printed with big, yellow sunflowers. On the blue-painted door hung a grapevine wreath decorated with a fake blue bird and a big yellow-and-white gingham bow.

"Very…homey," Mark said, studying the effect with a bemused expression.

She smiled. "Wait until you see the inside of the house. It looks like it was decorated by Aunt Bea from Mayberry. Everything Mother owns has a picture of either a chicken or a cat on it."

He was still smiling when the door opened.

"Rachel." Gillian Madison stood framed in the doorway, posing for maximum effect as she greeted her daughter and her guest. Her strawberry blonde hair was perfectly arranged in a sleek bob that framed her face, still quite young-looking at fifty-one. Her eyes were the same gray-blue as Rachel's own. She wore a blue blouse with a deep V-neckline, and close-fitting black slacks that weren't overly flattering to her full hips, but no one would have the nerve to tell her. "I'm so glad you could make it this evening. I know how busy your schedule is."

So her mother was in one of her dramatic moods this evening. She made it sound as if she hadn't seen Rachel in months, when it had only been a few days. Deciding not to play along, Rachel said simply, "Mother, this is my friend, Mark Thomas. Mark, my mother, Gillian Madison."

Mark turned on the charm. "It's very nice to meet you, Mrs. Madison. Thank you for allowing me to come this evening. Rachel told me you're a wonderful cook."

Predictably, Gillian looked delighted by his courtesy. "Well, aren't you nice. Come on inside, you two, and say hello to everyone else. They're all waiting for you."

That had been a subtle dig that they were the last to arrive, Rachel realized. They weren't late; it was actually exactly the time her mother had requested that they appear, but that was im-material, of course.

She and Mark followed her mother to the living room. She saw Mark take in all the country kitsch surrounding them in the house—the gingham and chintzes, the birdhouses and ceramics, the baskets and afghans and braided rugs and rooster art. And when he gave her a tiny smile, she knew he was comparing her mother's decor to her own sleekly modern style, or the casual chic designs she had presented to him. Dani said she always felt as though she were "drowning in cuteness" when she entered their mother's house, but both sisters agreed that it somehow suited Gillian.

As if she knew Rachel had just thought of her, Dani turned when they entered the living room. Rachel was the first to admit that Dani was the beauty in the family. Her long, honey-brown hair fell in waves to her shoulders, framing a face that had earned more than her share of male attention. Her eyes were a darker blue than Rachel's, and framed with impossibly long dark lashes that were entirely her own. Her figure was close to perfect, and shown to advantage in a clingy silk blouse and flowing slacks. She greeted Rachel with a faint smile, then narrowed her eyes as she studied Mark.

Nineteen-year-old Clay was draped on the couch with teenage bonelessness, his shaggy brown hair obscuring half his face, a sad little attempt at a goatee on his chin. Wires trailed from the earbuds that piped music from the player in his hand. Their grandmother had once asked if those earbuds had been surgically implanted.

Grandma, herself, sat in a chair across the room with a celebrity gossip magazine in her hands. An older version of her daughter, Martha Lawrence was just below average in height, broad-hipped and in good condition considering she had recently celebrated her eightieth birthday. She set the magazine aside when Rachel and Mark entered the room, her eyes focused on Mark from behind the lenses of her gold-plastic-framed glasses.

Rachel introduced Mark to everyone. Clay responded with a mutter, Dani with a distracted smile and Grandma Lawrence with a "Nice to meet you, young man."

"It's a pleasure to meet you, too, Mrs. Lawrence."

"Nice manners," Grandma approved with a nod. "How long have you been seeing my granddaughter?"

"Not very long." He looked completely at ease beneath her scrutiny, reminding Rachel that as a physician specializing in geriatrics, he spent most of his working days with senior citizens.

"But you're already coming to dinner with her family. Pretty brave of you."

He chuckled. "I'm looking forward to getting to know everyone."

"When's dinner going to be ready, Mom?" Clay asked impatiently. "I've got plans for later."

His mother frowned. "It will be ready in a few minutes. Take those things out of your ears, please. You can make an effort to be sociable until dinner's over."

He sighed heavily, but pulled the buds from his ears. He didn't often openly defy their mother, but Rachel was concerned that her brother was growing more distant and sullen. She worried that he was running with a crowd that was a bad influence on him while he was still at loose ends after high school, trying to decide what he wanted to do with the rest of his life. Though he had taken a couple of general education courses at a local junior college last year, he was currently on summer break, working part-time stocking shelves at a home improvement store, and spending the rest of his time hanging with an ever-shifting crowd of equally aimless young people.

Their mother turned toward the doorway. "I'll go put the finishing touches on dinner. Everyone behave yourself while I'm gone. Especially you, Mother."

Grandma Lawrence chuckled. "I'll try. Have the rest of you read this magazine? Can you believe what that little blond heiress has gone and done now? I swear, that girl's walking proof that money can't buy class."

Motioning to Mark to take a seat, Rachel murmured, "Sorry. Grandma's sort of obsessed with celebrity gossip."

"Well, that should keep the conversation moving," he replied with a smile. "The celebrities give her plenty to gossip about."

As if to prove his point, Grandma Lawrence launched into a tongue-clucking diatribe about the latest scandal involving a young heartthrob television star, pretty well monopolizing the conversation until they were summoned to the dining room.

Chapter Five

"So, Mark, what do you do for a living?" Rachel's grandmother asked almost as soon as they sat down in the big, family dining room.

Mark glanced up from his plate of roast beef and vegetables with a smile. "I'm a physician. Family practice, with a specialty in geriatrics."

As he had expected, the older woman's eyes lit up. "Is that right? You look awfully young to be a doctor."

He knew what she was fishing for. "I'm thirty-two."

"Really? You don't look it."

"Thank you. I think."

"Oh, it's a compliment. Think you can tell me what's wrong with my left foot? It aches all the time and no doctor's been able to make it stop yet."

"Mother," Gillian muttered with a shake of her head. "Not at the table."

"And why not? It's not like I asked him about my—"

"Don't ask him *any* medical questions at dinner. Let the man eat in peace."

"I'd be happy to talk to you about your foot after dinner," Mark said quickly when it appeared as though the older woman was prepared to continue the argument. "Maybe I can give you some suggestions. If not, I have a couple of friends who might be able to help you. I'd be happy to make a referral."

Looking pleased, Grandma Lawrence nodded. "Now that's real nice of you, young man. I like this one, Rachel. He's much nicer than that lawyer you brought home a while back. That young man was entirely too full of himself."

Rachel looked more resigned than embarrassed as she shook her head. "Yes, I know, Grandma. You made your feelings about Rex quite clear."

"Rex was a jerk," Clay muttered.

"I thought he was nice enough," Gillian weighed in.

"You just thought he was cute," Dani muttered with a roll of her eyes.

"Well, he was," Gillian replied shamelessly.

Rachel cleared her throat. "Okay, we can change the subject now. How was work today, Clay?"

Her brother ducked his head to feign intense interest in his meal and muttered something unintelligible around a mouthful of food.

"Answer your sister, Clay," Gillian ordered with a frown. "She asked you a question."

Clay heaved a resigned sigh. "I got fired."

"Fired!" Everyone except Mark repeated the word in stunned unison.

Clay sank lower in his chair. "It wasn't my fault."

"What did you do?" Dani demanded, apparently unconvinced by his comment.

"I told you, it wasn't my fault. This other dude, Randy, he's been pushing me around ever since I started working there. You know, mouthing off, getting in little shoves when no one else was looking, trying to make me look bad. He was pulling that crap again today and I just got tired of it. I started yelling at him to back off or I was going to make him regret messing with me, and the boss heard and he fired both of us for 'not being team players.' One of my friends tried to take up for me and tell him it was all Randy's fault, but old Pritchard wouldn't listen."

"Oh, Clay."

His mother's sad tone made his shoulders hunch even more. "It wasn't my fault."

"So what are you going to do now?" his grandmother asked.

"Look for another job, I guess."

"That's not going to be so easy without any references," Dani said, making no effort at tact. "This is the second time you've been fired. And the other time *was* your fault, because you just couldn't get to work on time."

"Shut up, Dani."

"Clay," his mother warned. "We have company."

"Yeah, well, tell her that."

Rachel gave Mark a look of apology. She looked very sorry she had initiated this topic, but how could she have known that her brother had lost his job that day? "I'm sure you'll find something else," she said to Clay.

Grandma Lawrence spoke up then. "Why don't *you* hire him, Rachel? I'd bet you have things Clay can do in your decorating and remodeling jobs."

Mark saw just a hint of a grimace cross Rachel's face. "Oh, I—"

"That's an excellent idea," their mother seconded immediately. "I was just going to suggest it, myself. I know you got him the job at the home improvement center, Rachel, but it would be so much better if he just works for you, especially after school starts again next month. You'd be more understanding of how much pressure he's under trying to find time for both work and his studies."

Pressure? From what Mark had already gleaned about the young man, he lived rent-free with his mother, who prepared his meals and paid for most of his expenses. Rachel had mentioned on the way to dinner that her brother usually took only two general education courses a semester. It hardly sounded to Mark like a life of pressure.

"I'll see if I can find something else for him," Rachel promised, as everyone seemed to have expected her to respond.

"I can start working for you Tuesday," Clay informed her. "I've got plans to go water-skiing tomorrow with some of my friends."

Nodding as if in satisfaction that Clay's employment situation was all settled, their mother changed the subject. "We're being rude to our guest to talk about all this family stuff. Tell us about yourself, Mark. Are you from this area originally?"

"I grew up in Georgia," he replied blandly. "This roast is delicious, Mrs. Madison. Best I've had in a long time."

She tittered in pleasure. "Thank you. Please, call me Gillian. Being called Mrs. Madison makes me feel old."

"It shouldn't," Mark responded gallantly. "You look as though you could be Rachel and Dani's older sister."

The trite comment should have elicited groans. Instead, Gillian blushed and giggled a little. "People tell me that all the time."

Grandma Lawrence gave her daughter a repressive look. "Oh, stop it, Gillian. You look exactly your age. Anyone who says differently is just trying to be nice."

Leaving her daughter scowling, the older woman turned her attention to Mark, who kept his expression carefully neutral. "Is your family still around here, Mark? You kin to any of the Thomases out Macon way?"

Reaching for his iced tea glass, he shook his head. "No. I don't have any family left in Georgia."

"Have you heard from Aunt Vivian lately, Mother?" Rachel asked, trying to change the subject for Mark's sake.

"Not lately. So, do you have any single brothers, Mark?"

He cleared his throat. "No." Not that he knew of, at least, he added in silent irony.

"That's a shame. I wish Dani could meet a nice, single young man like you."

Dani dropped her fork with a clatter. "Mother!"

"It was just a comment," Gillian replied with an exaggerated innocence.

"You *know* I have a boyfriend. He would be here with us now if you weren't so hateful to him every time I bring him around."

"I simply said I wish you could meet a nice single man. I can hardly think of Kurt as your boyfriend, since he's probably at home dining with his wife right now."

"Oh, man," Clay muttered, hiding his face behind his hair.

Grandma Lawrence sighed heavily. Dani's face flooded with heat, while Rachel just looked mortified. So much for her theory that her family wouldn't quarrel in front of a guest.

"That," Dani said through gritted teeth, "was uncalled for. *Especially* in front of company."

Gillian had the grace to look a little sheepish. "You're right. I'm sorry, Mark. Please forgive my terrible manners."

Before he could brush off the incident and quickly change the subject, Dani made a sound of angry exasperation. "You're apologizing to *him?* I'm the one you insulted!"

"You're also the one who reminded me that we have a guest."

"Would you two please—"

Ignoring Rachel's attempt to intervene, Dani snapped, "Oh, sure. You welcome Rachel's boyfriends at your table. After all, she dates lawyers and doctors and other big shots. I'm involved with a lowly car salesman."

"I have nothing against any honest profession," Gillian said coolly. "But at least Rachel doesn't date married men."

"She has a point there, Danielle," Grandma Lawrence piped in, not helping in the least. "Nothing good can come from taking up with a married man. If he cheated on one wife, he'll cheat on the next one, too."

"We can talk about this later," Rachel tried again. "For now, let's just finish our meal and—"

Dani turned on her sister then. "I asked you to talk to Mother and explain about Kurt and me. You said you would assure her that Kurt's getting a divorce and that he's really a great guy."

"I never actually said—"

"Rachel isn't going to condone this relationship," Gillian argued. "I asked her to explain to you what a mistake you're making with Kurt, didn't I, Rachel?"

Mark wondered if they always put Rachel in the middle of this sort of thing. He suspected they did. Just as everyone had simply expected her to rectify Clay's unemployment crisis.

Noting the signs of stress around her mouth, he decided it was time to see what he could do to help her. "I wonder if I could trouble you for a refill of this iced tea, Gillian. It's so good."

Instantly distracted, she jumped to her feet. "Of course. I'll be right back."

Without bothering to ask if anyone else wanted anything, she bustled out of the dining room with his almost-empty glass. Mark spoke then to Dani. "Rachel told me you're a very talented singer, Dani. She said you perform regularly at the Cantina de la Luna? I haven't been there in a long time, but I'll have to come soon to hear you sing. When do you perform next?"

"I'm there the first and third weekend of every month," she replied, tossing her head as she tried to get past her temper. "I've been performing there for almost six months. I'm the most popular singer they've ever booked."

"And the most modest," Clay muttered.

"Don't even start," Rachel warned, pointing a finger at her brother.

He shoveled the last of his food into his mouth. "I've really gotta go. The guys are expecting me."

"You can stay for dessert," his mother said as she set a refilled iced tea glass in front of Mark. "I made blackberry cobbler. Your favorite."

"But, I—" A look from her made him subside with a sigh of impatience. "Okay. But I've got to make it quick."

Mark could almost sympathize with the kid.

Rachel and Mark had just buckled themselves into her SUV an hour after dinner when her cell phone rang. She thought about ignoring it, but since it gave her an excuse to put off making her apology to Mark for the way her family had acted that evening, she muttered an apology to him and answered the call.

"I shouldn't even be speaking to you after the way you brushed me off last night," her ex-husband began without bothering with pleasantries.

She almost told him that she wouldn't have lost any sleep if he had stopped speaking to her, but she managed to refrain. "What do you want, Robbie?"

"Can you come by sometime tomorrow to look at my schedules with me? Maybe you can help me arrange things a little more efficiently so that the workload is spread out more evenly. You were always good at that sort of thing."

"Tomorrow?"

"If you can work me into your schedule," he said, just a hint of sullenness creeping into his voice again.

"I'll try to come by sometime in the morning," she replied in resignation. She remembered that she and Mark were supposed to start shopping for his house the next afternoon—if he still wanted to work with her after meeting her family.

"I don't suppose you can hostess for me next Friday night?"

"Don't push your luck, Robbie."

He sighed heavily in her ear. "I'll see you tomorrow."

"Fine." She disconnected the call without bothering to say good-night.

"I'm sorry," she said, starting the engine. "I'll let voice mail pick up if it rings again."

"Hey, I understand about having an overactive cell phone. Mine will start buzzing again when I start working at the clinic. You don't have to apologize to me because you had to schedule an appointment for tomorrow morning."

"I just wish it *had* been work related," she said with a light sigh. "That was my ex. He needs me to help him organize the work schedule for his restaurant."

"I see."

It was obvious that he didn't really see, but Rachel saw no need for further explanations about her dysfunctional relationship with her ex-husband. He'd had enough dealings with her barely functional family that evening. "It was nice of you to look at Grandma's foot after dinner. I doubt that you really wanted to end your evening that way."

"I didn't mind. But there was really nothing I could do for her except to recommend a couple of good orthopedists. I suspect she'll be advised to take anti-inflammatory meds and wear more supportive shoes."

Rachel smiled. "Grandma hates what she calls 'old lady shoes.' She only thinks of herself as a senior citizen when it's convenient for her to do so."

"I believe there are some decent shoe inserts that don't have to be worn with traditional 'old lady shoes.' If there are, I have no doubt that your grandmother will find them. She seems to be…resourceful."

"She is that."

"I always wanted a grandma. I pictured someone very much like yours, sweet-smiled and sharp-tongued. Maybe that's why I went into geriatric medicine."

"I love my grandmother dearly—even though she drives me

crazy sometimes. Just like the rest of my family. We're actually quite close, despite the impression to the contrary that you must have gotten this evening."

"No, I could tell you're all close. Your mother and sister are simply at odds right now about her boyfriend."

"And if it wasn't that, it would be something else. Mother and Dani have always clashed over everything, from cleaning her room when she was a kid to her clothes and curfews when she was a teenager to the decisions she has made as an adult. It's just the nature of their relationship. They're too much alike, I think."

"Have you ever considered telling them to work out their own problems?"

"I tell them that all the time. But they just keep dragging me in until I finally help them work something out. I don't know about this time, though. As long as Dani's seeing Kurt, and as long as he's married, Mother's going to be very vocal about her disapproval."

"I suppose you can't really blame her."

"I don't blame her at all. I actually agree with her. I just don't think nagging is going to change Dani's mind."

"So what would you advise her? To pretend she approves?"

"No, of course not. But she doesn't have to keep harping on her disapproval when she's already made it abundantly clear. In the long run, Dani's going to have to make her own mistakes."

Mark looked skeptical. "If it were my daughter, I don't think I could just stand by and let her make that kind of mistake without trying to do something about it. Of course, I'd probably just find the guy and pound him. I suppose your mother can't do that."

Hearing him talk about his hypothetical daughter took her aback for a moment, but she recovered quickly. "Well…no. Though Clay offered, I think. But it's still Dani's life. She's over twenty-one. All we can do is be there to pick up the pieces when this romance crashes—as it undoubtedly will."

"And have you picked up the pieces before?"

She responded with a humorless laugh. "You could say that."

He reached over to brush a strand of hair away from her cheek. "Do you ever get tired of being the caretaker?"

There should probably be a law against driving under the influence of Mark Thomas, she thought, forcing herself to concentrate on the road ahead even though that light brush of his hand had addled her senses. "It's just one of the costs of being a responsible chick, I guess."

He laughed. "A responsible chick?"

"Yeah. That's what my friend Kristy and I always called ourselves. Always the designated drivers, always the ones who get called in a last-minute crisis, the ones who get asked for 'just one little favor.' And I'm whining," she said with a rueful shake of her head. "Sorry. Guess my family got on my nerves more than I realized this evening."

"You aren't whining. You're tired. Between my family stuff and yours, you've been running all weekend. Why don't you come in when we get to my place and I'll make you some relaxing herbal tea? It's one thing I just happen to have in my kitchen."

She knew she shouldn't. But it was still relatively early. And they could talk a little more about his decorating…

"That sounds nice," she said, making the turn onto his street. "I can stay just for a little while."

From the corner of her eye, she saw Mark smile in satisfaction.

Amid the bustle of a popular diner, Mark faced Ethan and Aislinn across another table, this time for the breakfast they'd agreed to share before the DNA tests. Ethan and Aislinn would be going straight to the airport from the lab, but they had an hour or so before their appointment, so they had time to linger over the meal.

Mark hoped he would come up with enough conversational filler to keep that hour from dragging awkwardly.

Fortunately, Aislinn seemed determined to do her part in that respect. As they waited for their food to be delivered to the table, she told Mark all about the sightseeing she and Ethan had done the day before. "I had such a good time," she added. "It was a perfect day."

He was pleased by the sincerity in her voice and expression, both because he genuinely liked her and because now he didn't have to feel so guilty about avoiding them yesterday if they'd had such a good time without him. "I'm glad you had fun. Atlanta has a lot of interesting things to do. I'll have to show you some of the other attractions next time you're in town."

"We'd like that," Aislinn assured him with a smiling glance at Ethan.

"So, what about you, Ethan? Did you enjoy the day as much as Aislinn did?"

"I'm not really into touristy stuff," Ethan replied with a slight shrug. "But I liked being with Aislinn."

His fiancée laughed softly as their server arrived with their meals.

"So, Mark," she said, still gamely keeping the conversation moving, "what do you do for fun when you're not doctoring? Do you have any interesting hobbies?"

"I'll be busy furnishing my new house for the next few weeks. But I like getting together with some of my friends for basketball and touch football games when we have time. And I like to fly-fish."

Ethan perked up then. "Trout?"

"Oh, yeah. There's some great trout fishing in the Toccoa River. You fish?"

"Every chance I get. Ever fished for rainbow in the Sipsey in Alabama?"

"No, I've never even been to Alabama."

"You'll have to visit us there," Aislinn said immediately. "Ethan has a beautiful riverside cabin. That's where we'll live after we're married, since his parents are there, and I have no family to hold me in Arkansas. I can set up a new cake decorating business in Alabama."

Ethan looked pleased by the prospect. And maybe Mark was

a little bit psychic, himself, because he suddenly predicted Ethan and Aislinn would have a long, happy life together there in the riverside cabin.

"Maybe I will visit you there sometime."

"Well, of course you will," Ethan said almost impatiently. "We're family."

Family. The word still sounded strange to him. It certainly seemed important to Ethan, though, despite Ethan's habitually gruff manner.

"I'm sure you and your brothers will find that you have several things in common as you spend time together," Aislinn commented. "Especially since you and Joel are both doctors."

Brothers. This conversation was loaded with words that had a powerful effect on him.

"Mom and Dad are the ones who are going to want to spend time with you," Ethan added. "Joel and I will be lucky to get a word in once Mom gets to you."

Mark took a couple of deep swallows of orange juice and, though he wasn't much of a drinker, almost wished for something stronger. He could have used a little courage—liquid or otherwise—to help him face the thought of meeting his parents.

Aislinn smiled sympathetically, as if she sensed what he was thinking. "I haven't spent much time with them, myself, but they're very easy to talk to. Nic—my friend and your sister-in-law—has grown very fond of them, and she had a bit of an awkward start with your mother."

He still thought of his mother as the woman whose funeral he had attended several years ago, but he kept that to himself as he asked, "They didn't hit it off at first?"

"Mom's always been overprotective of us, especially since you disappeared," Ethan explained. "Joel was married before, and Mom was very close to his first wife. Heather died in a car wreck only a few months after she and Joel married, and it was hard on the whole family."

Ethan exchanged a look with Aislinn that Mark couldn't quite interpret. The Brannon family had certainly known their share of tragedy, he mused somberly. "I'm very sorry to hear that."

Ethan nodded, then continued, "Anyway, Nic is very different from Heather. Almost a direct opposite. Mom implied pretty blatantly that Joel and Nic weren't suited for one another, and Nic was understandably perturbed by that. Joel finally figured out that Mom was a little afraid to get too close to Nic because Nic's job as a police officer occasionally puts her at risk. Mom didn't want Joel to lose someone he loved again—and she didn't want to take that risk again, herself."

"Understandable," Mark murmured.

"Joel and Nic convinced Elaine that, though there are some inherent risks involved, being a cop in a relatively small town isn't terribly dangerous. Since then, Nic's won Mom over completely—just as she has the rest of us."

"She sounds like an interesting person."

"She's very special," Aislinn murmured. "Leaving Nic is going to be the hardest part about moving to Alabama. She and I have been as close as sisters for most of our lives."

"After we're married, you'll be sisters," Ethan reminded her.

Her smile brightened her already stunning face. "That's true. I'll still see her quite often."

"As often as you want," her doting fiancé assured her.

"I hope we get a chance to see Rachel again, too," Aislinn said with a rather arch look at Mark. "I really liked her."

He wondered if she already knew whether she would see Rachel again. He had a sudden urge to ask her about his future, if any, with Rachel, but he suppressed the impulse. Even if he fully believed in Aislinn's so-called psychic abilities, he thought it would be rude to expect her to perform on request as if she were a storefront seer with a rent-by-the-hour crystal ball.

Besides, the sheer anticipation of seeing Rachel again, not knowing what would happen the next time they were together, was all that was keeping him from obsessing about the overwhelming changes occurring in his life. He still felt his pulse trip every time he remembered the kisses they had shared after coffee at his place last night, before she had pulled away with what he'd hoped had been reluctance and promised she'd see him today.

He didn't like remembering that she was meeting her ex-husband this morning, even if she had assured him that it was strictly business. "I hope you'll get to see her again, too."

Aislinn studied his face for a moment with a slight frown, then gave him a sudden, reassuring smile. "Don't worry, she doesn't have feelings for him."

"Um—who?"

"The man she's meeting with this morning."

Mark looked at Ethan, who shrugged and smiled ruefully. "Don't ask me how she does it. But you can bet it's true. The fact that you and I are sitting here now proves that."

Shaking his head, Mark pulled the left corner of his mouth in a slight grimace of bemusement. "It'll take some getting used to."

An odd sound from Ethan made both Aislinn and Mark look at him in question. "What is it?" Aislinn asked.

Ethan cleared his throat. "That expression Ky—er, Mark just made? The way he twisted his mouth? He did that when he was little. I remember, we used to tease him just to see it. It's funny, I haven't thought of that in years, but, man, seeing him do it now…"

Mark squirmed self-consciously in his seat.

"Sorry," Ethan said. "I always hate it when Mom starts reminiscing about things I did as a toddler. I promise I won't make a habit of it with you."

"I'd appreciate it."

"Because I know it would make both of you gag, I won't mention that I found it very sweet that you remembered that," Aislinn commented with a little smile.

Now Ethan was the one who looked embarrassed. "We'd both appreciate it."

She laughed and, after a moment, Mark laughed with her. Ethan smiled tolerantly at both of them and then glanced at his watch. "We should probably go soon so we aren't late for our lab appointment. Not that I have any doubt what the tests will show."

Mark's amusement faded. "I'm sure you're right, but I still think we should take care of the formalities."

Ethan nodded. "And you still want me to wait to tell the rest of the family."

"Yes."

"I still don't agree with you on that."

"I know. And I know it's going to be difficult for you. But I need this, okay?"

"I've already given you my word."

Mark thought he'd already come to know his older brother well enough to believe that he kept his promises. "Thank you, Ethan."

Ethan signaled for the waiter to bring their check. "Yeah, well, you owe me. Everyone's going to be mad at me for holding out on them for so long. I'm blaming it all on you. Just like Joel and I always used to do when something mysteriously turned up broken around the house."

Mark supposed such reminiscences were going to be inevitable, especially when the whole Brannon family converged on him. It still felt strange, though, to hear stories about himself during a time he had no memory of now.

He wondered if he would ever truly feel a connection to that part of his life.

Chapter Six

"What about this one, Mark? It's rather nice, don't you think? It would look good in your bedroom lounge."

"Hmm? Oh, yeah, it's okay. Don't really like the arms, though."

Standing in front of the couch she had just pointed out, Rachel turned to him with her hands planted on her hips. "You're distracted again. We can't pick out a couch if you aren't paying attention. This is the centerpiece of your room, as far as furnishings go. You don't want to end up with something you hate."

He held up both hands and smiled. "Don't scold me. I'm paying attention. I just said I don't like the arms of that one, didn't I?"

"You did," she conceded. "And that's good, because it gives me an idea about what you like—but you still don't seem to be concentrating entirely on our shopping."

"How can I think about couches and tables when you look so pretty today? I really like you in green. It's my new favorite color, I think."

"And now you're trying to distract *me*," she chided, though she couldn't seem to resist smoothing a hand down the mint-green sundress that looked so nice with her soft brown hair. She had dressed for the summer heat, leaving her creamy arms and legs bare, and yet her dress and wedge sandals still managed to look polished and professional for their shopping outing.

"You're thinking about your breakfast with Ethan and Aislinn, aren't you? Are you sure there isn't something you didn't tell me? Did either of them do or say anything that upset you?"

"No, nothing happened other than the conversation I told you about. It was rather awkward at times, but not particularly upsetting."

"How did it feel saying goodbye to Ethan after the tests?"

"I'm not sure what you mean. It isn't as if I'll never see him again. Assuming that the tests come back positive, I'll be seeing Ethan—and the rest of the Brannon family—fairly soon, I expect."

"Is that what's bothering you? You're worried about meeting the rest of the family? Your parents?"

He skidded mentally away from the thought of meeting his parents. This wasn't the time to dwell on that daunting prospect.

"I'll concentrate," he promised, dragging his gaze away from her to look around the showroom floor. "What about that couch over there? It's nice."

She didn't seem entirely satisfied with the sudden change of topic, but she cooperated. "Yes, that one does have nice lines, but it's too large for the space. Maybe we can—wait a minute. How about this one?"

"It looks comfortable, but kind of bland, isn't it?"

Rachel shook her head indulgently. "We'd have it covered in something other than this natural-colored fabric, of course. I'm thinking a cranberry red to go with the red accents we're using through the rest of the house, like the walls in the dining room. Several throw pillows in coordinating stripes and prints."

He circled the couch, noting the thick, inviting cushions and narrow rolled arms. "I like the little wood blocks at the bottom."

"The exposed wood feet? Yes, I like that feature, too."

Sitting on the couch, he tested the comfort of the double cushions. They felt good, but he didn't plan to be sitting upright on this couch that often. Swinging his legs around, he stretched out, keeping his shoes off the fabric. "Yeah, I could watch TV pretty comfortably on this."

"You like to watch TV lying down?"

"It's been called my TV sprawl."

She laughed. "Then you should definitely test for sprawl-ability."

Settling his head more comfortably on the rolled arm, he replied, "This one sprawls pretty good. Cranberry red, huh?"

"We can look at fabric samples while we're here. But cranberry was the color I chose in the sketches I showed you."

"And I liked it. Go for it." He straightened and pushed himself to his feet. "This will do. I assume it fits the budget we worked up. Do I pay now or will they bill me?"

She blinked at him. "You want to buy this one? Mark, it's the first couch you've looked at."

"No, it's the third. You showed me the one with the funky arms, then I pointed at the one that didn't fit the space, and then you found this one. I stretched out on it, and it felt good. No need to waste time looking at a bunch of others if this one works. What do we look at next? Chairs?"

Laughing, she threw up her hands. "Apparently, this job isn't going to take as long as I originally thought."

"That's what I'm thinking," he assured her, giving the couch a proprietary pat.

"Then, by all means, let's look at chairs."

He grinned, delighted by her. "Lead on."

They wandered through the crowded showrooms, looking at chairs of every shape, size and color, though Mark was still having a hard time not looking at Rachel. They had to pause several times for her to answer her cell phone, after he assured her that he didn't mind her taking calls. She did receive a lot of calls, and since he was accustomed to hanging out with other doctors who always had a phone or a pager nearby, that was saying something.

He couldn't help noticing that only about a third of her calls were business related. The others seemed to be from various members of her family needing advice or asking questions or just wanting to see if she was free to chat. She handled each call quickly and efficiently, causing few delays in the furniture shopping. He could tell she was thoroughly accustomed to multitasking.

"Here's a contender," she said after they'd studied and rejected several options. She rested her hand on the back of a low, upholstered armchair with the same rounded arms as the couch he'd selected. "It would look good in a bold stripe."

"It's nice—"

"—but not what you have in mind," she finished for him.

He tried to envision himself sitting comfortably in his lounge in that chair with a book. "No. Not quite."

"No problem. There's another over here that looks interesting."

Following her, he made a valiant effort not to focus on the soft sway of her hips. Pulling his gaze away with an effort, he found himself distracted by a chair on the other side of the room from the one Rachel was moving toward. He headed that way, thinking he could just take a quick look and then rejoin her.

Shortly afterward, she stood in front of him, her hands on her hips again. "Here you are. I thought you were right behind me."

"I was. And then I got sidetracked." He settled more deeply into the impossibly soft leather armchair, feeling it wrap around him like a warm, welcoming hug.

His face must have revealed his thoughts. "Like that one, do you?"

He let his head fall back against the leather. "Oh, yeah."

"Comfy?"

"I'm thinking about spending the rest of the day right here."

"You wouldn't get much shopping done that way."

He closed his eyes and smiled. "Not sure I'd care."

"That must really be a comfortable chair."

"Want to try it?"

"Think you can get out of it long enough?"

"Maybe. But only because I like you."

She laughed and dropped into the chair after he moved out of it. "I like you, too. And, oh, wow, this chair is amazingly comfortable."

Standing in front of her, he smiled smugly. "Didn't I tell you?"

"Yes, and you were absolutely right."

"So, can I have it?"

She laughed. "Of course you can have it. It's your house."

"I meant, does it go with the couch?"

"We hadn't considered leather, but this chair goes quite nicely with the couch. We'll have it done in a warm caramel leather, if you like, and then pull the colors together with the throw pillows and other accessories."

"Works for me. Now what? Tables?"

She laughed again as she stood. "I've worked with some fast shoppers in my time, but I think you take the cake. You're really sure you don't want to take some more time to think about these things? You'll potentially have to live with them for several years, you know."

He shrugged. "Nice couch. Great chair. Why would I need to look anymore?"

"I've got a couple of other clients I'd like to introduce you to," she said with a faint sigh. "One woman has been trying to decide on a lamp for almost three months. I've shown her hundreds, but she hasn't liked any of them."

"Seriously? A lamp?"

"One lamp. Not even a particularly noticeable lamp. It's in a back corner of her library. But, for some reason, she has decided it's a Very Important Lamp, and so it must be the perfect lamp. I'm about to wash my hands of it. We should finish her remodel by the end of next week, and if she hasn't picked a lamp by then, she's on her own with it."

"You won't have to worry about that sort of thing with me. I just want my house finished, even though I want stuff I like, of course. But I can't imagine getting that emotional about a lamp."

She shrugged. "It's probably some sort of Freudian thing. Though I only had one psych class in college, so I'm hardly qualified to analyze the meaning of lamp neuroses."

"You're not much into psychology, I take it?"

"Oh, I'm interested in people. Just not the science of studying them. I don't think most people fit into tidy checklists of person-ality types, you know? I have a friend who majored in psy-chology in college and is always trying to analyze people, even though she went into retail instead of therapy for a career. She owns a gift shop in Buckhead. Anyway, she calls me a 'classic type A' personality with a somewhat obsessive need to take care of other people's problems."

Because that sounded reasonable to Mark, considering what he knew of Rachel so far, he asked cautiously, "How do you feel about that description?"

She had paused to look at a console table that was much too stark for Mark's taste. "It's far too simplistic. I'm type A only when under deadline—which, I admit, is fairly often—and while I'll confess I have a hard time saying no when my friends and family ask for favors, I can do so when necessary. It isn't an ob-session, I just like to help people out when I can. What's wrong with that?"

Her defensive tone made him smile. It sounded as though she and her friend had argued about this on many occasions. "There's nothing wrong with that, as long as you leave time for a life of your own."

She cleared her throat. "Well, of course I do that. Do you like this console table to go behind the couch you selected?"

"No."

His blunt response made her laugh again. "Okay, we'll look at some more. You definitely know what you like."

"Definitely," he murmured, unable to resist giving her a quick once-over.

She shook a finger at him in teasing warning and pulled him along to another display of tables that were much more to his liking.

After a couple more hours of shopping, Mark insisted on taking a coffee break. They popped into one of the ubiquitous chain stores, where Rachel ordered a low-cal vanilla latte and Mark chose café au lait with skim milk and a big white-chocolate-chip-and-macadamia-nut cookie that he insisted on splitting with her.

"We could use the sugar rush," he assured her. "We worked off the calories hiking around that huge store."

She didn't need much convincing. She loved cookies of any type, especially macadamia nut. She broke off a tiny piece of her half and popped it in her mouth, her way of making the treat last longer. "Mmm. Good."

"We've gotten a lot so far today, haven't we? I like the tables we found for the lounge. Good idea of yours to use the two small square tables in place of one big coffee table. I'm going to like that look."

"I do, too. And I really love that fold-down desk with the glass-doored hutch you discovered. It will be perfect on the wall between the two dormer windows."

"Yeah, I like the idea of having a writing surface in the lounge, even though my formal office will be downstairs. I thought that piece was nice with all the shelves on top for books and the little cubbyholes behind the drop-down desk. That part made me think of an old rolltop desk."

"We could still find antiques for you," she reminded him. "There are some wonderful pieces in local stores."

He shook his head. "I'm fine with reproductions for now. I

don't have a lot of sentiment about old things, though I appreciate the workmanship of the old handmade pieces. Besides, it would take too long to scour antique stores. I like one- or two-stop shopping."

"Instant gratification."

He grinned, and her heart beat a little faster in response to the flash of white teeth. "What can I say? I'm the impatient sort. What would your friend the wannabe shrink say about that?"

"I have no idea. But I'm sure we'll both hear her conclusions when you meet her."

He nodded. "I like the idea of meeting your friends. I have a few I'd like you to meet, too."

She sipped her coffee to avoid having to come up with an immediate response. They were moving a little fast here, what with meeting each other's families and now talking about meeting their friends. Perhaps it was another indication of Mark's impatience, his tendency to see something he wanted and move straight in to claim it. Which made her take another gulp of coffee and almost choke on it.

"Are you okay?"

She nodded, dabbing at her watering eyes with the corner of a brown paper napkin. "I guess it went down the wrong way."

"Maybe we can do some of the antique stores when we're looking for, you know, sit-around stuff. Things to put on the shelves in the hutch and other places that need decorating," he suggested. "That might be fun."

"Yes, it would be. I love antique stores. We'll also use some of the items you already own, that are in those boxes in the spare bedroom. I know you have a few things you'd like to display. Maybe some photographs we can put in nice frames?"

His smile faded, and the light in his green eyes suddenly seemed to dim. "I don't have any photographs I want on display."

"Oh. I'm sorry, I—"

"No." He shook his head apologetically. "*I'm* sorry. I didn't mean to snap at you. It's just—well, the only family photos I have are of me and…"

"And your mother," she finished for him.

"The woman I thought was my mother," he corrected her, looking bitter now.

"She must have loved you, Mark."

"She did. Obsessively, it seems. Enough to steal me from a family who also loved me. How could she do that, Rachel? How could *anyone* do that?"

The raw pain in his voice made her heart ache for him. It was the first glimpse he'd allowed her of the torment he'd been secretly feeling since Ethan Brannon had appeared at his door with the truth. She reached out instinctively, intending to cover his hand with hers, but he pulled away before she could touch him.

"No," he said, his expression masked again now. "We're not going to talk about that now. I'm ready to shop again. Maybe we could look at furniture for the den, since we've ordered most of the pieces for the bedroom and lounge?"

She tried not to be hurt that he'd shut her out so quickly and so completely. As if he regretted letting his emotional barriers slip in front of her, even though he had just implied that he wanted their lives to become even more entwined. What sort of relationship did he think they could have if they weren't completely open with one another—or was *she* the one in danger of rushing things now?

Trying to hide her feelings as well as he did, she followed his conversational lead. "The sectional I showed you in my presentation is at another furniture store. We can go there when we leave here if you like."

"It looked great in the picture, but I'd like to try it out for comfort."

"I think you'll find that it has the same degree of sprawl-ability as the last one you liked."

The smile was back in his eyes when he replied, "Sounds good to me."

* * *

Aislinn had left her car in long-term parking at Little Rock National Airport when she had flown to Alabama a few days earlier to tell Ethan she'd discovered where he could find his missing brother. It seemed as if it had been longer, she thought as they walked side by side across the parking lot. When she'd left Little Rock, she and Ethan had been estranged because of his reluctance to let her into his battle-scarred heart. Now they were engaged to be married and he'd been reunited with his brother. It was hard to imagine that so much had happened in so short a time.

"I'm glad you decided to come here with me for a day or two," she said when they reached her car. "I know you need to get back to work soon."

"We both do," he said with a shrug. "Your employees are probably struggling to keep up since you've been gone."

"They are," she agreed with a grimace. "I've got a lot of late nights to put in to fulfill all my obligations for the next few weeks. I was just lucky I didn't have any weddings scheduled for this past weekend. Only a golden anniversary party, and my assistant was able to handle the very simple cake they ordered."

Throwing his bag in her trunk, he asked, "How long will it take to arrange everything so you can move to Alabama?"

"A couple of months, probably. We should be able to be married by fall."

He scowled. "That long?"

Her fiancé was the impatient sort. Once he'd made up his mind to do something, he didn't like having to wait around. She sensed that it was a trait all the Brannon brothers shared. "I'll get everything settled as quickly as I can," she promised.

"We haven't really talked about the wedding, itself. Uh—do you want one of those big, fancy affairs? Because if you do, it's okay."

Her heart melted a little in response to that awkward offer. She knew how much Ethan would hate a "big, fancy" wedding, and yet he was willing to tolerate one. For her.

"No," she assured him quietly. "I don't want a big wedding. For one thing, I have no family to invite. We could elope, just the two of us and a justice of the peace, but I think your mother would be very disappointed if we did that. Why don't we just plan something small, just your family and closest friends, if you like? We could have it out on your deck overlooking the river. That would be lovely."

"Now, see? This is why you're perfect for me," he said, visibly relieved. "We can have it in mid-September, and the weather should be perfect."

"Make it the third weekend in September," she said, feeling the familiar tingle that always accompanied her insights. "It's going to rain the second weekend."

"Um, yeah, okay. The third Saturday in September. Perfect."

He was growing more and more comfortable with her gift, just as she was, finally, after so many years of fighting and then denying who she was. Perhaps that was why her predictions seemed to be getting somewhat stronger—Ethan had freed her to be herself.

She started her car. "You're staying at my place, aren't you?"

"Of course. I'll see Joel tomorrow after he gets off work for the day."

She could tell by his tone that he looked forward to being with Joel again. The brother with whom he had shared his life, rather than the near stranger who still looked at him with a not-so-hidden wariness in his eyes. "It's going to be hard for you to spend time with Joel and not tell him about Mark."

"Yes, it is. Harder than with Mom and Dad, actually, because Joel can almost always tell when I'm not being straight with him."

"But you aren't going to tell him?"

"I promised Mark I wouldn't until we get the results of the DNA test back. But—it's not going to be easy."

"It's going to be a huge adjustment for your family, having him returned to them at this stage. They don't know Mark Thomas, and he doesn't think of himself as Kyle Brannon."

"I know. It *will* be strange. I feel bad for him. I'd hate to have people suddenly appearing in my life, expecting things from me that I didn't know how to give, wanting me to be someone I'm not."

"You don't expect anything from him," she pointed out.

"I guess not. But it will be different for Mom and Dad. They still love him. Yet to him, they're just a couple of strangers."

"What about you, Ethan? How do you feel about him?"

He was silent for a long time. And then he said, "He seemed like a nice enough guy. I'm glad he didn't turn out to be a criminal or a bum or anything, which could have happened, considering. But—do I have the same feelings for him that I do for Joel? No, of course I don't. He's not the little kid I knew for such a short time. I hope we can be friends, eventually, but I don't know if we'll ever really be brothers. And I hate that."

"I'm sorry. For all of you."

"I know. But I'm being self-centered, aren't I? You didn't even get the chance to meet your mother."

A ripple of pain went through her, but she suppressed it quickly. "She left me behind a long time ago. Intentionally— unlike your brother, who had the choice made for him. She knew where I was for all these years if she'd wanted to get to know me. She said in the letter she left me that she wasn't proud of the things she had done, but that she still believed she'd made the right decision to leave me with my grandfather. She wasn't cut out to be a mother, and she couldn't have given me the stable, comparatively normal life I had with my grandfather and my great-aunt."

"So, what do you think?" he asked after a pause. "Will Rachel be joining the family, too?"

Aislinn frowned as she gave a moment of thought to his question. "I don't know. Rachel and Mark both have some individual issues they'll have to deal with before they can go much further as a couple. And to be honest, I'm not sure they'll be able to work things out."

"Yeah? Shame. They seemed like a good match."

"I think they could be—but I'm just not sure it's going to happen. At this point, I wouldn't be surprised either way."

"So, how about us? You see us making our match last?"

He was teasing, but she heard the sincerity in his question. "You know I'm never very accurate making predictions about myself. But I don't think it takes any extrasensory ability at all to foresee that you and I are going to make our relationship work. We're both too stubborn to concede defeat once we set our minds—and our hearts—to a goal."

He chuckled. "Then there's no doubt at all, is there? Because both my mind and my heart are fully committed to spending the rest of my life with you."

She glanced away from the road ahead just long enough to give him a loving smile. "That makes two of us."

Chapter Seven

"We got a lot done in four hours," Mark said, glancing at his watch in satisfaction. "All we need now are linens and some sit-around stuff, and I'll have a finished bedroom suite."

Rachel was still amused by his gung ho attitude, even after spending the afternoon with him. "If we keep going at this pace, your house will be finished inside a month."

"Works for me. Now that we've finished decorating for the day, why don't we go have a drink somewhere? Maybe stretch it into a nice dinner?"

"I would love to," she said, "but I can't tonight."

She was gratified that he looked disappointed, even after they'd spent so much time together over the last few days. "I guess I have been sort of monopolizing you lately."

She smiled up at him as they stood beside her car in the furniture store parking lot. "You haven't heard me complaining, have you?"

A breeze-tossed strand of hair tickled her cheek. Mark

reached up to brush it back. The slight shiver that coursed through her had nothing to do with the air temperature, since it was a very warm summer afternoon. And she wasn't complaining at all.

"I completely understand that you have a life of your own," he assured her. "I just enjoy spending time with you."

She had never had time to play coy dating games. She answered him candidly, "I like being with you, too. And if I hadn't already agreed to help Robbie tonight, I would definitely have taken you up on your offer of a drink."

His smile changed, just a little. His tone was ultracasual when he asked, "Robbie? Your ex?"

"Yes. His wife is sick—again—and he needs me to fill in for her at the hostess desk in his restaurant. It's what I used to do when we were married, and sometimes he asks me to help out when he gets really shorthanded. I keep telling him he's going to have to find someone permanent to fill that position, but Kaylee keeps telling him it isn't necessary, that she'll be able to handle everything as soon as she's over her latest bout of…"

She stopped herself before she could say the word *hypochondria*. She tried not to be openly critical of her ex-husband's wife. She wouldn't want anyone to get the mistaken impression that she was in any way jealous of Kaylee or that she still had any lingering feelings for Robbie, other than an often-exasperated affection.

"Of whatever," she amended lamely.

"So Robbie hires you to fill in as hostess whenever his wife is ill?"

"He doesn't exactly hire me," she said, uncomfortable with the word. "I mean, I'm doing well with my business, so I don't need to moonlight. I just help him out occasionally when he gets in a bind."

And when he nagged her to the point that it was easier to just do it than to keep arguing with him, a tiny voice inside her gibed.

"I see."

He wouldn't be the first man she'd dated during the past couple of years who couldn't understand Robbie's continued dependence on her. "I'd better go. I'll see you in the morning, okay?"

He ran his fingertips along the side of her jaw. "Would it be incredibly unprofessional of me to give my decorator a good-night kiss in the parking lot of a furniture store?"

"Oh, extremely," she assured him, already rising on tiptoe to tilt her face toward him.

His mouth hovering only a breath away from hers, he asked, "Does that mean I should try to resist?"

"You can try," she said, slipping her arms around his neck and pulling his smiling mouth down to hers.

Robbie's Restaurant was hardly an example of creative or modest naming. He'd called it that even though he and Rachel had still been married when he'd opened it, and she'd been part owner of the business. Truth be told, she'd been the one who'd put in the most hours of planning, organization and old-fashioned sweat equity to get the place up and running, but when he'd confided that he'd always wanted to see his name on a restaurant marquee, she'd happily conceded.

She had always wanted Robbie to be happy. Even when he had come to her in tears less than a year after they'd opened the restaurant to tell her that he'd fallen in love with one of their waitresses, she had quietly taken herself out of the way of his new romance. They had filed for a quick, amicable divorce in which their assets had been divided in a way that slightly benefited him—as had so much of their marriage—but not so much that Rachel felt the need to fight him. She hadn't wanted his restaurant. By then, she had just wanted out.

Even at the time, she had suspected that the reason she'd been so agreeable to the split was because she'd been secretly aware for some time that she'd married Robbie for all the wrong reasons, allowing herself to be persuaded by his pleas and mistaking fondness for lasting love.

He'd married Kaylee a few months later, and the two of them had spent the past almost-three years bickering, separating, getting back together and turning to Rachel for sympathy and support. For some reason, Kaylee had decided that Rachel was like a surrogate sister to her, always available with a shoulder to cry on or a helping hand to offer. Granted, it was an awkward situation, but Rachel had learned to live with it. She actually rather liked Kaylee, in the same resigned, often bewildered way she cared for Robbie.

"Hello, Rachel. I see Robbie conned you into working again tonight."

Pulling two menus out of a wooden rack, Rachel smiled at the longtime customer who had greeted her. "Good evening, Mr. Belleci. It's nice to see you again."

"You, too, Rachel. This is my niece, Anna, from Denver. She's in town for a conference and I had to bring her to my favorite restaurant while she's here."

Nodding pleasantly toward the tall, fashionably thin young woman who looked as though there were things she would rather be doing than dining with her charming, but undeniably talkative sixty-year-old uncle, Rachel motioned toward one of the waitstaff. "Mary will see you to your table. And she'll make sure that you both get a cocktail on the house to welcome your niece to our city."

Beaming, the portly man patted Rachel's arm on his way past. "That's why I keep coming back here, Anna. Nicest bunch of folks you'll ever meet. Even though Kaylee gets a little curt when things get busy," he added pointedly over his shoulder to Rachel.

Kaylee did not thrive under pressure, Rachel thought with a wince, which made her less than ideal to serve as hostess on particularly busy evenings. She believed Kaylee really had tried, but she was making more and more excuses to avoid her responsibilities lately. Yet, when Rachel had suggested that Kaylee turn over the hostess position to someone else, she had resisted that, too.

Rachel secretly believed that Kaylee liked being seen as the co-owner of the place where she had once been just a part-time server. And maybe she was a little concerned that if she stayed away too long, Robbie would notice one of the younger, new servers who now worked in the restaurant.

Rachel had tried to assure Kaylee that it wouldn't happen, but she didn't think Kaylee was convinced. After all, that was how Robbie and Kaylee had become a couple.

Was Grandma Lawrence right? Once a cheater, always a cheater? Despite the way her marriage had ended, Rachel didn't want to believe that of Robbie.

As if in response to her thoughts of him, Robbie appeared in front of her. She studied him dispassionately, noting that he'd spent a little extra time tonight arranging his glossy chestnut hair in an attempt to hide the widening bald spot at the top of his head. He was a moderately attractive man, though not nearly as striking as Mark, of course. Buff and spray-tanned, he still looked a bit older than his thirty-two years, maybe because of the perpetual frown lines around his pale blue eyes.

"Kind of a slow night," he grumbled, looking around the empty entryway.

She shrugged. "It's a Monday. And it's past the dinner rush."

"I really appreciate you coming in tonight, Rach. I promise, I won't ask again. Kaylee promised she'd be back tomorrow night."

"You really are going to have to hire someone else, Robbie. Kaylee can't be here every night even when she's feeling well."

"She doesn't work on Wednesday nights," he argued defensively, even though they were both aware that Rachel already knew the schedules. "Some of the other employees take turns filling in for her then. It's just that everyone had other responsibilities tonight."

"I've told you that's really not a practical plan. You and Kaylee need to make out a schedule for how many nights a week she wants to work, and which nights those should be. The other nights, you need a reliable, regular host or hostess to establish a relationship with your clientele. I've been telling you both this for months, but you haven't been listening."

"I'll talk to Kaylee," he muttered. "Not that she'll listen. Everything I think we should do, she takes the opposite opinion just to be stubborn."

"I'm sure that's not true," Rachel replied, even though she couldn't speak with complete confidence that there wasn't a grain of truth to his remark.

"You were always so much easier to work with than Kaylee," he said wistfully.

That was because she had pretty much given in to anything he'd wanted, just to keep him happy, Rachel thought ruefully. Being as spoiled as Robbie, Kaylee wasn't so accommodating. "Yes, well, you and Kaylee will work things out. You always do."

"Maybe you could have dinner with us Wednesday night? Our way of thanking you for your help tonight. And maybe during dinner we could talk about some of your ideas for restructuring the work schedule. Kaylee will be more likely to listen with an open mind if it comes from you rather than me."

"Thank you for the invitation, Robbie, but I'm going to have to pass. I've got a very busy week ahead. Besides, you and Kaylee don't need me to help you with your business plans. I have no investment in the restaurant anymore, remember? Maybe you should hire a small business consultant. I actually met someone who does that recently, perhaps you should contact him about his rates and services."

Robbie's mouth turned downward in a familiar, rather sulky frown. "You seem to be busy a lot lately."

She glanced at the front door, wishing a customer would come in to distract him. "It's called a life. I have one."

"So what about this new guy you're seeing? Is it serious?"

"I'm not going to discuss my social life with you, Robbie. Especially not here."

His frown deepened, as if he'd read more in her expression than she had intended to reveal. "I know you've dated some since you and I split, but this one seems a little different. You've never taken anyone home to meet your family so soon before."

She stared up at him. "How did you know about that?"

"I ran into Dani at the post office this morning. She said you brought the guy to Sunday dinner. And she said it looked serious to her. She said she didn't remember you looking at anyone else quite like you do this guy."

"Sounds like she said a lot," Rachel muttered grimly.

"She's concerned about you. After all, you haven't known this man very long. I know you get lonely, Rachel," he added with a melting sympathy that set her teeth on edge, "but you really should be careful about getting involved with the wrong sort. Just because he's a doctor doesn't mean he's the right man for you. Remember how badly things turned out with that lawyer."

Things hadn't worked out with "that lawyer" for several reasons, primarily because she hadn't been all that interested in him. It hadn't helped that the constant demands of her family and ex-husband had come between them so often. But she had been entirely serious when she'd told Robbie she wasn't going to discuss her dating life with him.

Looking him directly in the eyes, she said in a low voice, "If you say one more word about this, I'm walking out that door and you're on your own for the rest of the evening. Is that clear enough?"

He blinked rapidly, backing down as he always did when Rachel showed a rare flash of temper. "Sorry. Just trying to help—the way you're always helping me, you know? Because we still care about each other."

"You'd better get back to work. And so should I. Good evening," she said brightly to the two smiling couples who were just entering the restaurant. "Party of four?"

* * *

"Maybe next time we can play at my house," Mark said to the three men sitting around the table with him Tuesday evening. "I might even have chairs to sit on within the next few weeks."

Emilio Rosales, Mark's friend and one of his new partners in the family practice clinic, grinned across at him. "I'm warning you, I expect snacks. And beer. Donna won't be catering our poker game at your place."

Mark popped a salsa-loaded chip into his mouth, chewed, swallowed, then said, "I'll come up with snacks. Won't be as good as Donna's cooking, but it'll be edible."

"When do you think you'll be finished with your house?" Adam Whalen asked, glancing up from the cards in his hand. "How much more do you have to do?"

"We picked out furniture for the master bedroom suite yesterday. Today we found most of the stuff for the den. Found a great game table to go in there."

"Comfortable chairs?" J.T. Crain wanted to know.

"Would I choose any other kind?"

Adam studied a tray of sweets, chose a chocolate-dipped cookie and asked before eating it, "What's it like working with a fancy decorator? Bonnie wanted to hire somebody when we bought our place, but I talked her into doing it herself. I laid it on pretty thick about how talented she is at that sort of thing and how she didn't need to pay someone to do something she could probably do better."

"Your wife is a good decorator," Mark replied with a shrug. "I'd never have come up with some of the ideas Rachel has for my place. She has a way of knowing exactly what I want, even though I don't know quite how to describe it, myself."

"Is she pretty?" Emilio asked.

Donna gave him a stern look as she carried in another bowl of salsa. "Is who pretty?"

"Mark's decorator," her husband replied, his expression studiously innocent. "I was just curious."

"What she looks like has nothing to do with whether she's good at her job. You should have asked if she's a talented designer."

"Mark's going out with her," Adam volunteered slyly.

"Really." Donna looked at Mark in sudden interest. "Is she pretty?"

Laughing, Mark replied, "Yes, she's pretty. *And* she's a talented designer."

"You'll bring her to dinner sometime?"

"We're still in the early stages of dating, but yeah, I'd like you guys to meet her." He suspected that he was falling too hard and too fast for Rachel, and he worried that this was entirely the wrong time to let himself get so involved. And yet…he wanted her to meet his friends. Wanted to become an important part of her life.

The fact that he'd spent last night prowling the empty rooms of his house and hating the image of her spending the evening with her ex-husband wasn't at all encouraging. It was good to spend this evening doing something more productive, especially since he hadn't yet told his friends about his newfound family and therefore didn't have to talk about them or even think about them for a few hours.

"So, are we going to play poker or gossip about decorating and dating?" J.T. complained, tapping the table with one finger.

Emilio picked up his cards. "We're playing poker."

Donna moved toward the doorway of the basement game room. "I'll be upstairs with Angelina. Let me know if you guys need anything, okay?"

"You don't have to wait on us, Donna," Mark chided her.

She smiled back at him. "I know. I like having company. Even if it's only Emilio's ruffian friends. Besides, my bridge club meets here three times a year, and I always make him wait on us. He looks very handsome in an apron."

Leaving the men laughing, she took her exit with that shot.

"You're a lucky man, Emilio," Mark commented, nodding toward a framed photo of Emilio, Donna and their two-year-old daughter.

Emilio tossed poker chips onto the pile in the center of the table. "Tell me about it."

"He's not the only one," Adam reminded them, never one to be outdone. "I count myself pretty lucky to have Bonnie and the boys."

"And I am a happily single guy who likes to play poker," J.T. growled. "If we could get past the *Oprah* hour?"

The others all laughed, and turned their attention back to the card game.

Rachel was just about to turn in Tuesday evening when her telephone rang. Assuming it was a member of her family, she sighed and glanced at the screen. Her frown turned to a smile when she recognized the number. "Hello?"

"Hi. I hope it isn't too late. You weren't in bed, were you?"

Just hearing Mark ask that question in his deep drawl made her body temperature rise by a degree or so. "No, not yet. Is everything okay?"

"Yes, fine. I tried to come up with a logical excuse to call you—some sort of decorating question or something—but the truth is, I just wanted to hear your voice one more time today. Is that freaky?"

Laughing, she slipped into bed and tucked the covers snugly around her, settling in for the call. "Not freaky at all. I'm glad you called."

"How was your meeting this evening?"

Even though he couldn't see her, she wrinkled her nose. "Boring. The speaker droned on for forty-five minutes. The worst part was that she only had about twenty minutes of interesting material. The rest was repetition."

"Ouch."

"Exactly. How was your poker game?"

"I left thirty dollars poorer than when I started."

"Ouch."

He laughed. "Exactly. But I had a great time."

"Then I suppose it was worth it."

"Oh, absolutely. I'll earn the money back next time. The luck tends to pass around among us."

"How long have you been playing poker with them?"

"Couple of years. I met Emilio first, through a professional organization. He brought me into the poker games to replace a guy who moved away, and we've all gotten to be pretty good friends since. We take turns meeting at each other's houses every other Tuesday."

"When's it supposed to be your turn again?"

"Not the next time, but the one after."

"Four weeks."

"Right."

"Then we'll just have to have your gathering room ready by then, won't we? You can't entertain your poker friends in an empty room."

"That would be great."

It was so easy to talk with Mark. He told her more about his poker friends, and she shared a couple of amusing anecdotes about the professional women's group that had sponsored the meeting that evening, and before she knew it more than half an hour had passed. It was getting quite late, but she was reluctant to end the call. It was almost like being back in school again, she thought with a smile—having a crush on a cute boy and talking on the phone until late at night.

She jumped when the telephone on her nightstand rang, suddenly and loudly, cutting into the cozy conversation with Mark. "Can you hold on a second?" she asked him.

"Sure, go ahead."

Caller ID informed her that it was her mother on the other end of the line, which worried her a bit since her mother was usually in bed by this hour. "Mother? Is everything okay?"

"Not really," her mother replied, her voice sounding strained. "Clay's been in a car accident. He's been taken to the hospital."

Chapter Eight

It would have been impossible for Rachel to be anything but beautiful, as far as Mark was concerned, but she was decidedly worn-looking when she showed up at his house Wednesday morning at the time they'd agreed on.

"Did you get any sleep at all last night?" he asked, drawing her inside.

"A couple hours." She pushed her hair out of her unusually pale face. "By the time I got Clay home and Mother calmed down and then got back to my apartment, I was so wired it took me a while to get to sleep."

"You should have taken the day off."

She shrugged. "I'd rather work. And speaking of which, I brought the catalogs I mentioned to you."

"I'll look at them. But first, is your brother okay?"

Her mouth tightened. "Yes, he's fine. Just a little banged up."

"Did he total his car?"

"Oh, he wasn't in his car. He was with a friend, who was

driving. Thankfully, Clay was in the passenger's seat. At least they were both wearing seat belts. That probably saved their lives."

"How did the accident happen?"

Her eyes darkened even more. "Kirby, Clay's friend, was driving too fast. Missed a turn."

"Were they drinking?" he asked quietly.

He watched her throat work with a swallow. "Yes," she admitted in a low voice. "They were."

"How much trouble is Clay in?"

"Not as much as Kirby, obviously, since he wasn't driving. But it wasn't pleasant. And Mother, of course, was very upset. Because she has a problem with night blindness, she can't see well enough to drive, so she was stuck at home fretting about whether Clay was hurt, and unable to get to him."

"So she called you."

"Of course."

She said it so simply, as if there had been no other option. And maybe in her family, there hadn't been.

She looked as though she didn't want to discuss this any further, and he supposed he didn't blame her. It wasn't as if her family troubles were any of his business. "You said you had some catalogs to show me?"

The relief he saw in her eyes let him know he'd been right about her desire to change the subject. "Yes. I've bookmarked a couple of items I think you'll like."

Leading her into the kitchen, where they could sit on the bar stools and spread the catalogs in front of them, he asked, "Would you like coffee? I just made a fresh pot."

"Oh, yes, thanks. The painters should be here shortly. I could use a caffeine jolt before they get started."

"Have you had anything to eat this morning?"

"I, um—yes, I'm sure I had something."

She couldn't remember. Which meant she probably hadn't.

"Sit down," he said, motioning toward the bar stools. "I'll get the coffee."

She looked a bit surprised when he set her cup and a plate holding a large, microwave-warmed muffin in front of her. "Just coffee would have been fine."

"You should eat something. It could be a while until we have time for a lunch break."

She broke off a bite of the muffin and popped it in her mouth. "Mmm. Good. Thank you."

She was so obviously unaccustomed to having someone take care of her. Which only made him want to do so even more. "I buy them at a little bakery a few blocks from here. You should taste their pastries. They're so good, I have to watch myself or I'd eat way too many of them."

Swallowing another bite of muffin, she opened a catalog to a page she'd marked with a bright blue sticky tag. "Okay, take a look at this—"

He scooted his stool closer to hers on the pretext of getting a better view of the page.

A week after Clay's accident, Rachel stood in the center of Mark's bedroom, surveying her work with satisfaction. Most of the lounge furnishings hadn't arrived yet, but the bedroom furniture had been in stock, so this room was pretty much finished. He'd slept in his new bed for the past couple of nights, reporting that it was quite comfortable, but she'd just finished adding the decorative touches to the room.

There were still spaces for Mark to add a few personal items he would collect in the future, but he no longer had to sleep in a room that felt bare or cold. Just the opposite, in fact, with its warm caramel walls and hand-rubbed mahogany furniture.

Her gaze moved from the dark-red-and-tan-figured Turkish rug on the floor to the massive platform bed with its paneled headboard and frame. The cranberry red that ran throughout his house was used here in awning-striped bedding, an assortment of pillows bringing more color into the room. Over the bed hung a painting Mark had spotted in a gallery on one of their shopping outings, a woodsy landscape with a glittering river running across it. Seeing it made him think of the happy hours he'd spent fly-fishing; he had purchased it with his usual brisk efficiency, spending less than ten minutes deciding if it was what he wanted.

She'd chosen mismatched nightstands, one an antique chest with carvings on the drawer fronts, the other a stand that matched the bed and dresser, with a shelf for books underneath the single drawer. Rather than using table lamps, she'd had swing-arm bronze sconce lights with natural linen shades installed on either side of the bed above the stands. The stands were uncluttered, holding only a few knickknacks that Mark had selected—a straight glass vase filled with bamboo stalks, a burled-cherry bowl, wood-and-brass candlesticks, a brass alarm clock. No photographs.

A double dresser on one wall was topped with a large, mahogany-framed mirror. Like the nightstands, the dresser was tidy, with only a bamboo tray on one end and a hand-carved hinged box on the other. A braided money tree plant in an Asian-inspired vase sat on the bamboo tray. The box held Mark's watches, cuff links and other small items.

A wooden storage chest sat at the foot of the bed to hold extra linens and blankets. The cushioned top gave Mark a place to sit and put on his socks and shoes. Between the room's two red-draped windows sat a mahogany tower chest for socks and under-wear and handkerchiefs, and a rectangular mahogany-framed floor mirror stood in the corner of the room on the other side of the dark granite fireplace.

More art hung on the walls and a potted green plant sat on the tower chest. The overall impression, she decided, was warm, earthy, secluded and serene—all words Mark had mentioned when describing the bedroom he wanted.

"It looks great. Really great." Mark entered through the bedroom door and stood looking around in visible pleasure.

She turned to greet him with a smile. "I didn't know you were back yet. How was your first day at the clinic?"

"Not bad. I only saw a few patients today, since I was just getting settled in." He made a slow three-sixty, shaking his head as he did so. "I can't get over how much you got done today. The linens, and the stuff on the walls, and the things on the nightstands—it just looks amazing."

"I'm glad you like it. The rest of your lounge furniture should arrive within the next few weeks. I know you'll be glad to have that done so you'll be able to crash in front of your TV in there."

"It will be nice, but in the meantime, I'm going to be very comfortable in here."

"Yes, I think you will. Oh, and did you go into the kitchen yet?"

He grinned. "Yes, I saw it. The breakfast room set arrived. I finally have a table to eat at."

She nodded. "The deliverymen arrived about an hour ago. They carried everything in and set it where I directed them to, but I haven't had a chance to decorate down there yet. I wanted to finish in here first."

"Where are your helpers today?"

"I've got everyone working on the Perkins remodel today. There wasn't really any heavy lifting to do here this afternoon, just some arranging and hanging, which I could handle myself."

"Did Clay show up for work this morning?"

She sighed. "Yes."

Her brother had skipped work yesterday, claiming he didn't feel well. Rachel had suspected that he was hungover again, despite the lectures he had endured from both her and their mother since the accident last week. Henry, Rachel's job foreman, was not happy with his new employee, but he'd promised to try to work with Clay.

"I'm sure he'll straighten up, Rachel. He's young, still a little immature. Trying to decide who he is. It's normal for him to test his limits some before he settles into a steady routine. He's got you and your mother to keep him grounded, so I doubt that he'll stray too far off."

"I hope you're right. I know he's still young, but he won't be nineteen forever. He needs to be going to school, training for a real career, not just fetching and carrying for Henry. Something tells me *you* weren't testing your limits at nineteen. You couldn't have wasted much time to have gotten your medical degree as young as you did."

Mark shrugged. "I never had much time to hang out with friends and get into trouble. I started working when I was fourteen to help my—to help pay the bills. I went to college on scholarships I couldn't afford to lose, so I was studying a lot at Clay's age."

She hadn't missed the stammer when he'd almost mentioned the woman who had raised him, but she let it go. "You had a goal even then—you wanted to be a doctor."

"Yeah. Like I said, I didn't have much extra time."

Maybe he didn't mean to imply that Clay had been overly indulged during the past few years, not required to work for his rent or bills or anything except personal spending money above what his mother regularly slipped him. She couldn't have argued with him too much if he'd said it outright. Clay *was* a bit spoiled. Their entire family had bent over backward to try to make up to him for the loss of his father at such an early age.

Still, her brother was a good kid, she assured herself firmly. And it *was* hard for him not having a father's guidance. They just had to be patient with him, and keep pointing out to him that he was in danger of wasting the best years of his life. He'd promised her last week that he would straighten up. That he would register for a heavier class load in the fall and choose a future career to train for. She believed him—but she couldn't help worrying…

"Let's go down and look at your breakfast room furniture,"

she said, abruptly changing the subject. "I've hardly had a chance to see it since it arrived."

He didn't move immediately toward the doorway. She looked up at him in question.

"I missed working with you today," he said.

They had spent nearly all of the past week together, shopping and making decorating decisions during the daytime, then dining and talking and ending the evenings with increasingly ardent kisses. They'd both had other commitments during the week, but when they were free, they ended up together. She wasn't complaining—but she was growing increasingly nervous about how close they were getting, and how fast.

This wasn't exactly an ideal time for either of them to get involved in a serious relationship. He had family issues, and so did she. He was starting a new job, and she was still getting her business firmly established. And yet…she suspected that any relationship with Mark could get serious very quickly.

"I'm sure you did more good taking care of sick senior citizens than helping me put linens on your bed."

His smile turned impish. "Maybe. But I would have loved dearly to help you make my bed. Or unmake it."

Even though her heart bumped hard, she gave him a chiding look. "Behave yourself. We said we were going to take this slowly, remember?"

"I know," he agreed a bit reluctantly. "Still, I can't help but fantasize occasionally."

Which, of course, made her heart pound harder at the thought of him fantasizing about her. She moistened her lips, trying to think of something clever to say.

A low sound escaped him as the smile slid off his face. His gaze was on her mouth now, his eyes darkened to a deep emerald. His head dipped toward hers, though he paused just short of their lips touching. Giving in to her own desire, she closed the distance herself.

His right hand closed into a fist at the back of her head, her hair caught between his fingers. His left hand settled at her hip, drawing her closer to him. It was getting more difficult for him to keep their kisses light and casual. She could tell by the tension in his body as he pressed her against him how much he was trying to hold back. The answering tautness in her own body was an indication of how unsuccessful she was at suppressing her reactions to him.

He kissed her again, his tongue dipping between her lips in a teasing, seductive way that made her ache for more. She was intensely aware that the freshly made bed was only a few steps away, and she imagined that Mark was thinking along those lines, as well. She had to admit it was tempting…but she just wasn't ready to take those steps.

She pressed both hands against his chest, a signal that she wanted him to back away. Well, she didn't exactly want him to, but her implication was clear.

His hand tightened in her hair for just a moment, but he didn't resist beyond that. Without bothering to hide his reluctance, he put a few inches of space between them.

"I'm trying," he said, his eyes locked with hers. There was a rough edge to his voice, and a dark wash of color on his cheeks, but he didn't look annoyed, just frustrated. "But it's getting more difficult."

She swallowed hard. "We've only known each other a few weeks. And we're still involved in a professional relationship. Despite evidence to the contrary, I don't usually mix business with personal involvement. It makes everything too complicated."

"It's already complicated." He slid a hand slowly down her arm, leaving a trail of tingles in his wake. And then he took another step backward. "But we'll take it at your speed. Let's go look at the breakfast room furniture. I need to get out of this room."

She noticed that he didn't look at the bed again as they left the room, though she couldn't help briefly glancing that way, herself.

* * *

The breakfast room table was round with a pedestal base. A matching buffet sat against the wall. Underneath the table lay a dhurrie rug with blue-and-gold medallions on a field of dark red. Five chairs surrounded the table, their wooden seats softened with red and dusty-blue plaid cushions. A bronze chandelier with little linen shades hung over the table, which was still bare, as was the buffet, since Rachel hadn't had a chance to decorate in this room yet.

Still, Mark was pleased to have a table. If necessary, he and the guys could play cards in here until the gathering room was finished, he thought.

A box in the corner of the kitchen held an assortment of items he and Rachel had picked up during a leisurely shopping outing earlier in the week. Focusing almost fiercely on her work, she put together a centerpiece made up of a mirrored base, a glass jar filled with river rocks and bamboo stalks, and a couple of glass candleholders. Bamboo place mats completed the table arrangement—all of which had taken her maybe fifteen minutes, he thought with an admiring shake of his head.

She moved to the buffet. "Since I didn't have my helpers with me today, I sweet-talked the delivery guys into helping me hang this heavy mirror," she said, her voice brisk and impersonal. "I think it looks great here. By reflecting the glass doors and the patio beyond, it makes the breakfast room look big and bright."

"It does look good," he agreed, though he was looking at her, and not the mirror.

She pretended not to notice as she set a pair of antique brass candlesticks on one end of the buffet, and a heavy footed brass bowl on the other end for fresh fruit. Three bright red pots planted with fresh herbs added color and fragrance when lined in front of the low mirror.

She chatted as she worked, telling him that he could use the buffet to store extra serving pieces and linens, and that he could easily change the look of the room occasionally with seasonal flowers and fruits or different-colored candles or place mats. He nodded as if he were paying close attention to her advice, rather than wishing they were back upstairs in his bedroom, trying out that comfortable new mattress.

She caught his attention again when she asked, "Did you hear from Ethan last night?"

"No," he said, pushing his hands into his pockets. "There was no need for him to call. I told him I'd let him know when the test results come in, and I'm not expecting them for another few days yet."

"I thought maybe the two of you would talk occasionally while you wait for the results. Get to know each other better, find out more about your family so you'll be ready to meet them when you let Ethan tell them about you."

He shrugged. "There's not much more to say right now. I'll deal with them when the time comes."

"You seem to be trying awfully hard to put your family out of your mind until it becomes necessary," she commented, glancing over her shoulder at him as she made a minute adjustment to the fruit bowl. "When are you going to want to talk about them? Or discuss your feelings about what happened to you?"

"Like I said, I'll deal with it once I get the test results back." He moved around the bar into the kitchen. "I think I'll make some coffee. Do you want a cup?"

After a brief pause, she shook her head. "No, thank you."

She stepped back to take a critical look at the buffet. "That looks good for now. I still need to finish your kitchen. We need some nice canisters and kitchen tools, and you have got to choose some better dishes than those mismatched pieces in your cabinet now. Then we…"

He was about to interrupt her almost-fevered rambling, but her cell phone beat him to it. It was the first time anyone had called her since he'd arrived just over half an hour earlier, he reflected wryly. That might have been some sort of record. Not only that, the call was actually about business this time. He could tell she was talking to her foreman, Henry, about the Perkins job, answering a few questions he had for the next day.

He glanced at his watch. It was just after five. He'd finished early at the clinic on this first day, giving himself a chance to settle in before he slid into his usual habit of working long hours.

"That's enough for today," he said when Rachel disconnected her call. "You've been at it for hours here, doing a great deal by yourself."

"There's not much more I can do today, anyway. We have some more deliveries scheduled for tomorrow, so I can do more then."

"I'll be leaving for hospital rounds early tomorrow, so you'll have to let yourself in." He had entrusted her with a key and his security codes, granting her full run of his house. It had felt a bit odd giving her the key. He would have done so even if she had just been the decorator, of course—but since it was Rachel, there had seemed to be a special significance to the exchange.

He couldn't imagine ever wanting to take the key back.

Standing at the end of the bar while the coffee brewed, he leaned one elbow against the granite surface. "Will you have dinner with me?"

She hesitated again, then said, "I think I'd better go tonight. I have some things I need to do at home."

Soberly studying her expression, he asked, "Running?"

She smiled a little crookedly, not bothering to deny it. "Maybe."

"I'm suddenly scary?"

She tucked a strand of hair behind her ear. "Not you, exactly."

"Then what?"

Twisting her fingers in front of her, she shrugged. "I just— you were right earlier. It *is* getting complicated."

Pushing away from the bar, he took a deliberate step toward her. "So what's the problem?"

"I work for you, Mark. You're paying me to decorate."

"Yes. Why does that matter? You aren't doing anything differently than you would for any other client, are you? As far as the work is concerned, I mean."

"No, of course not. I'm following the decorating plan we drew up from the beginning. I'm not trying to take advantage of our…friendship when it comes to business."

Friendship. Not the word he would have chosen. Though he liked to think he and Rachel were already friends, he'd made no secret that he wanted much more with her. "So…do you think I'm trying to take advantage of *you?* Using our business association for personal reasons?"

"No, of course not."

He took another step, which brought him within a few inches of her. "If you don't want to see me on a personal level, just say so, Rachel. I won't pressure you. It won't affect our working relationship. I can be entirely professional, if that's what you want."

She started to speak, then fell silent, biting her lower lip. Finally she replied in a rueful voice, "I don't think that would work."

"You don't believe I'd keep my distance?"

A near smile touched her lips then, though it held little amusement. "I trust you. But I'm not at all sure I trust myself."

There was that frankness again that he'd come to expect from her. It both bemused and captivated him. "What does that mean, exactly?"

She sighed. "It means that every time you touch me, I lose my capacity to think rationally. All you have to do is smile at me and I want to just toss my decorating plans aside and drag you to the nearest flat surface. I'm not used to that, Mark. Everything is different with you. And it seems too soon to feel that way."

He would have given anything to be able to smile at her at that moment, just to find himself dragged to the nearest flat surface. The new table, the granite countertop, the floor—it didn't really matter where. But just picturing that outcome made his muscles go rigid, his jaw clenching with the restraint he was exerting to keep himself from reaching out to her. "Rachel—"

"You did ask."

"Yeah," he agreed huskily. "I asked."

"So…I'd better leave. Before this gets any more complicated—or awkward—than it already is."

He touched her arm when she would have passed him. He didn't hold on, but she stopped, anyway, her eyes locked with his. "Don't go."

She moistened her lips, leaving them moist and glittering and making his heart thud even harder in his chest. And then, after what felt like a very long time, she sighed and moved into his arms, pressing those soft, wet lips to his.

The bed was as comfortable as Mark had said. Rachel sank into the mattress when he laid her back on it, the pillow-top surface just cushy enough. The new sheets were still crisp, but luxuriously soft. She noted those details only briefly before Mark came down on top of her and all thoughts of anything but him evaporated.

His mouth was on hers, his hands wandering over her body. She spread her palms across his bare back, loving the warmth, the strength, the ridges of muscle and bone beneath his smooth skin. He moved his lips to her throat, and she closed her eyes and arched her head, denying him nothing.

She had tried to resist him, to resist herself—but she couldn't remember now why she'd even made the effort. She'd known from the first time she and Mark had met that he was special, that something was going to happen between them. Maybe she didn't have Aislinn's talent for seeing the future, but it hadn't taken extrasensory perception to interpret the way her hand had tingled the first time he'd taken it in his, or the way his eyes had narrowed with interest when she had smiled up at him. Certain signs were age-old. Instantly recognizable.

In this case, irresistible.

They rolled, and now she was the one with unlimited access. She nibbled his jaw, tasted his neck, wriggled down to trace a line across his broad, sleek chest with the tip of her tongue. That made him groan—which made her smile.

He smothered that smile with his lips as he rolled again, tumbling her beneath him. Wrapping her arms around his neck, she opened herself to him. Completely. But even as he joined their bodies, she had a troubling feeling that he was holding something of himself back from her.

Chapter Nine

A strand of hair was tickling his nose. It took almost all of Mark's energy to reach up and move it aside even as Rachel nestled more snugly into his shoulder. Dropping a light kiss on the top of her head, he stroked her arm lazily as he stared up at the ceiling, every cell in his body relaxed and sated.

Well, maybe there was something else he could use, he thought with a very slight frown. "Rachel?"

"Mmm?" She sounded as if she were drifting, not quite asleep but not fully awake, either.

"Are you hungry?"

Stirring a little, she murmured, "I don't know. Maybe."

"I'm hungry. Lunch was a long time ago."

She lifted her head then, smiling down at him. Her eyes were smoky, more gray than blue now, her brown hair tousled around her still-flushed face. He had to make a concentrated effort not to let himself be distracted again. "You're pretty much always hungry, aren't you?" she teased.

"At least three times a day. Why don't I go downstairs and find us something we can eat up here? I think I can provide a mattress picnic."

"I can help you make something."

"No." Tangling his hand in her hair, he brought her face to his for a lingering kiss. "I like seeing you here in my bed."

She laughed softly. "I can't stay here indefinitely."

"No," he agreed reluctantly. "But you can stay for another few hours, can't you?"

"I suppose so." This time she was the one who initiated a kiss, making it a thorough one. "Don't be gone long," she whispered when she drew back.

Clearing his throat, he said hoarsely, "I won't be."

He pushed himself out of bed, reaching for his blue-striped boxers. He figured those and his white T-shirt would be enough clothing for now. He didn't plan to wear them long, he thought in anticipation, heading downstairs with a last, lingering look at Rachel.

He realized he was whistling when he opened the refrigerator door to look inside. He stopped with a sheepish laugh. What was he going to do next, break into a song-and-dance routine? One would think he was a young man who'd just made love for the first time.

Oddly enough, he felt almost as though he had.

He was falling hard, he acknowledged, pulling deli containers out of the fridge. Right on the edge of tumbling all the way, if he hadn't already. He should probably be scared. Weren't single guys supposed to be apprehensive when they came this close to losing their hearts? But all he felt was eager to explore the next stage with her.

Inventorying the tray he'd assembled, he studied the chicken salad, baguettes, cheese cubes, raw veggies and tiny ginger cookies, things he'd picked up on the way home that evening. He'd hoped to share them with Rachel, though he hadn't gone as far as picturing them eating in bed. This was even better, he thought, adding a bottle of wine and two glasses to the tray. He remembered napkins, plates and flatware at the last moment, then couldn't think of anything else to add. He didn't have a lot of experience at entertaining or preparing meals. He hoped this would do.

Balancing the tray carefully between his hands, he made his way up the stairs, telling himself he would look like a real bozo if he dropped the whole thing on the way up. Maybe they should turn out the lights and burn some of the candles she had arranged around his bedroom, he mused. That would be a romantic gesture that might make up for any shortcomings in the menu.

He pictured Rachel lying in his bed in candlelight, her hair spread on his pillows, her eyes heavy-lidded. He almost dropped the tray again. Steadying himself with a self-recriminating frown, he walked into the bedroom.

Only to find Rachel fully dressed and sitting on the bench, donning her shoes.

He came to a stop, dishes rattling on the tray as she looked up at him apologetically.

"You're leaving," he said unnecessarily.

She stood. "I got a call."

"Of course you did." He set the tray on the bed. "Is it an emergency? Is there anything you need?"

"It isn't an emergency, exactly. Mother and Dani got into it again, and Mother's upset. I could tell she needed me to come calm her down."

If he'd had pockets, he would have stuck his hands in them to keep himself from reaching out to her. Too aware that he was standing there barefoot in a T-shirt and boxers while Rachel looked ready for a business meeting, he crossed his arms over his chest and tucked his hands into his elbows. "Well, then I guess you should go."

She hesitated, searching his face. "You're annoyed."

"No." It was a lie, of course. He *was* a little annoyed, as much with himself for feeling that way as he was with her. He was being selfish, he told himself. Her mother needed her. He had no right to try to interfere. "I'm just sorry you have to go."

She took a step toward him and placed her hand against the side of his face. "I'm sorry, too."

Catching her hand in his, he placed a kiss in her palm. "Call me if there's anything I can do for you."

"I can't think of anything, but thank you for offering." She glanced at the bed, biting her lip when she studied the tray he'd put together so carefully for them. "I'm sorry," she whispered again.

"It's okay. Go take care of your mother."

She paused only a moment longer, then turned and walked out of the room, her cell phone in her hand.

Mark didn't bother to see her out. He sank to the edge of the bed and reached for the tray, deciding he might as well eat, even though his appetite had faded considerably.

"Rachel, are you listening? You seem a thousand miles away."

Glancing up from the plate of food she'd been toying with, Rachel looked at her mother, who sat across the kitchen table from her. "I'm listening. You were talking about how worried you are that Dani's going to be hurt."

"She is, you know. I'm not just being hysterical or overcontrolling. I don't trust that Kurt. He treats her very badly, and she doesn't seem to see that."

"I know." She set down her fork and reached for her tea glass. "I don't like the situation, either, but you have to admit there isn't much we can do about it. And the more you try to talk her out of seeing him, the more determined she is to continue. Kurt has some sort of hold on her that we can't exactly understand. All we can do is hope she comes to her senses soon."

Her mother didn't look particularly reassured by the words Rachel had said so many times before. "I just pray that she doesn't wait until it's too late."

Rachel frowned in response to something she heard in her mother's voice. "What do you mean? You don't think Kurt's actually dangerous or anything, do you? I mean, sure, he's a cheat and a liar, but we've never had any indication that he physically mistreats her."

Her mother bit her lip.

"Mother?"

Shaking her head, she replied, "No, I don't know anything for certain. I just…have a bad feeling about him. I've only seen him a couple of times, and those encounters were very brief, but I just didn't like what I saw."

Rachel had seen the guy even less than her mother. She knew he was handsome, slick, charming in a trying-too-hard sort of way. "I confess I didn't like him much, but I never saw anything dangerous in him. Why haven't you said anything about this before?"

"You know how you all accuse me of being overly dramatic. I didn't think you would take me seriously. But there's something in the way Dani's been acting lately that scares me a little. She's too wrapped up in this man. Too determined to prove me wrong about him. I'm afraid she would stay with him as much out of pride as love now, even if he is treating her badly."

"Dani would never let any man abuse her. She's got too much self-respect for that." At least, she wanted to believe that.

Like the rest of the family, Dani had had a difficult time coming to terms with her father's untimely and unexpected death. Rachel had been the eldest, the one expected to be the achiever and the leader, and Clay had been the baby. The young prince. But Dani had been Daddy's little girl. Rachel suspected Dani had been trying to find that sort of unconditional male approval ever since her father's death, though no one had seemed to give her what she needed. Until she'd met Kurt and thrown herself impetuously into an imprudent love affair.

"I hope you're right," their worried mother murmured. "Will you try talking to her again, Rachel? Maybe this time you'll get through."

"Or maybe she and I will get into a fight and she'll stop talking to me altogether."

"I don't know. Maybe you're right. She won't even listen to your grandmother on this one and you know she's always respected what her Grandma Lawrence had to say."

"You're just going to have to let this go, Mother. At least for a while. Or unless you have some concrete evidence that Kurt is a physical threat to Dani."

"I'm trying," she replied with a sigh. "That's why I asked you over tonight. To remind me that I can't control this situation, no matter how much I might want to try."

"Well, I hope I'm succeeding in that."

Her mother made a little sound of resignation. "Maybe a little. Oh, well. I hope you didn't have other plans for the evening."

It was the first time she'd even asked, Rachel realized. Thinking of Mark standing by his bed with a tray of food in his hands, looking so tousled and sexy in his T-shirt and boxers, she swallowed hard. "No. No real plans."

"Good. Is something wrong with your meal? You said you haven't had dinner, but you've barely touched your food."

She glanced down at the chicken and rice concoction on her plate. "I guess I'm just not very hungry tonight."

To appease her mother, she picked up a homemade yeast roll and broke off a corner of it, sticking it in her mouth and washing it down with a sip of iced tea.

Rousing herself a little, her mother asked, "So, how's your big decorating job for Dr. Thomas coming along?"

Relieved that the subject had turned to herself for a change rather than her trouble-prone sister, she replied, "It's going very well. I got a lot done today."

"Did your brother help you? Has he been working hard this week?"

"Um—yes, I suppose. He doesn't work directly with me, you know. I have him on the Perkins job, tearing out walls and pulling up carpet."

Frowning, her mother said, "That doesn't sound like very pleasant work. It isn't dangerous, is it? Clay's awfully young to be tearing down houses."

"He's almost twenty. I have a couple of guys younger than Clay who work for me occasionally. And he isn't tearing down the house, only helping take down a few walls so we can open up the floor plan. But I guess he's pulling his weight, though of course he didn't work yesterday."

"What do you mean, he didn't work yesterday? He left here yesterday morning saying he was going to work."

Rachel swallowed a groan. Now she'd done it, set her mother off again. But how could she have known Clay had lied to her? And how stupid was Clay to have done so, she thought irritably, when there was every chance that he'd get caught? He was working for his sister, for Pete's sake!

Now her mother was carrying on again, lamenting the fact that she was such a terrible mother that two of her children were making such poor choices. Sure, Rachel had turned out all right, but Rachel had always been the responsible, dependable type. And besides, Rachel had been grown when her father had died, whereas her younger siblings had still been in need of a man's guidance.

Feeling vaguely as if she'd just been termed boring, Rachel assured her mother that she was a perfectly wonderful parent and that it wasn't her fault that Dani and Clay were being so reckless lately. After all, they were both adults, even if Clay was still a teenager for a few more weeks. If she privately believed her mother had spoiled both of them a little, she kept that to herself. Both her sister and her brother were too old to use that as an excuse for their behavior much longer.

"I'll talk to Clay," she said wearily, pushing her hair out of her face. It had been a very long day. A life-altering day, actually.

She was really too tired to deal with this tonight. But she would. Just as she always did.

She wouldn't mention her own deepening involvement with Mark. She wasn't quite ready to talk about it, for one thing, and her mother certainly didn't need to hear about it tonight. Maybe she felt just a little bit isolated right now, despite her large family. But that was probably just a momentary bout of self-centeredness that she would have to overcome.

She had other people to take care of now. Beginning with her distraught mother.

"I really believe you've been avoiding us lately, Ethan," his mother scolded him over dessert and coffee Friday evening. "Every time I've asked you over lately, you've had an excuse."

Finishing the last bite of his dessert after the hearty meal she had served, Ethan pushed his plate away with a muffled groan. He was too full, but he'd eaten every bite of the meal as a sort of amends that he had been avoiding his parents lately. "I've been working. Trying to get far enough ahead that I can take Aislinn on a three-week honeymoon."

Mentioning the honeymoon accomplished what he had intended, making his mother go all misty and starry-eyed.

"Three weeks," Lou Brennan said with a harrumph. "Your mother and I could only take a week for a honeymoon when we got married. We had to get back to work."

"Yes, well, we were younger. Didn't have as much money put away as Ethan does," Elaine pointed out. "I think it's wonderful that he and Aislinn are going to have that time together, especially since they're having to spend so much time apart now while she prepares to sell her house and her business in Arkansas. Have you decided where you're going to take her yet, Ethan?"

"We've decided to go to Ireland. Since both of our families came from there originally, we thought it would be an interesting trip."

"Oh, how romantic," Elaine breathed. "I've always wanted to go to Ireland."

"You said you wanted to go to Paris," her husband reminded her. "Isn't that where we've agreed to go next spring?"

"I've always wanted to see Paris, too," she retorted.

His mother had longed to travel for the past several years, Ethan reflected. Lou, however, was not one to enjoy leaving home. He was perfectly content to practice orthodontia during the day and putter around the house in the evenings and on weekends. He liked gardening, working in his wood shop and spending hours searching for signs of termite infestation—something he had yet to find, but which he was convinced was only a matter of time. To Elaine's delight, he had finally agreed to take her on that European vacation she had always wanted.

"Do both," he suggested, knowing he was going to get a look from his dad, but figuring it would be worth it. "Go to Paris *and* Ireland. Since you'll be over there, anyway, you might as well get your money's worth out of the trip."

He was right about the frown from his father, but his mom's face lit up like a lantern. "That's a wonderful idea. Isn't it, Lou?"

"Sounds expensive."

"You can afford it, Dad. Besides, you told me once that you wouldn't mind seeing Ireland."

"When did I say that?"

"When I did that genealogy report in high school. We were talking about where our ancestors came from, and you said you wouldn't mind visiting Ireland sometime."

"That was a long time ago."

"Thanks, Dad, I'm not *that* old."

"I'm going to go look on the computer right now and find a travel plan that includes both Paris and Ireland," Elaine announced, pushing her chair away from the table. "You guys just stack your plates in the dishwasher when you're finished."

She bustled out of the room, determination radiating from

every inch of her petite body, leaving Ethan to be frowned at by his father.

"Well, you've set her off now," Lou complained as he gathered his dessert dishes and moved toward the dishwasher. "This vacation's going to cost me a fortune. Not to mention all the time I'll have to take off from work."

"Wouldn't hurt you to cut back some," Ethan replied with a shrug, following his father from the table. "I'm not suggesting you retire yet, you'd hate that, but you can work fewer hours and spend more time with Mom."

"Yeah, I guess I could," his father conceded. "She has been a little restless lately. Her volunteer work doesn't seem to satisfy her like it used to. Maybe it's just with Joel married and you about to be married yourself, she's feeling empty-nest syndrome all over again. I know it's been a long time since you boys moved out, but it's different thinking of you as married with new families of your own."

Ethan poured the last of the coffee into his cup, then rinsed the carafe and wiped the counter with a paper towel, saying as he worked, "I don't see how that could be so bad. She's getting two great daughters-in-law, and I know Joel and Nic are planning to have kids soon. Guess Aislinn and I will be talking about that, too. Mom's going to be a fantastic grandmother."

"She will, won't she? And I like to think I'll be a pretty good grandpa."

"Absolutely."

Smiling in satisfaction at the prospect, Lou took a moment to consider it, then sighed. "I think part of the problem might be the anniversary that passed this year. It's been thirty years now, you know. He'd have been thirty-two his last birthday."

Having been in the process of lifting his cup to his mouth, Ethan jerked, spilling hot coffee over his hand. Cursing beneath his breath, he ran cold water over his hand, then bent to clean up his mess with another paper towel.

His father moved closer in concern. "You okay? Did you burn yourself?"

"I'm fine. Just clumsy."

Lou set a hand on Ethan's shoulder. "It's hard for all of us to think about Kyle, son."

This, of course, was why Ethan had been making himself scarce lately. He hated keeping the knowledge of Mark's existence to himself when it would mean so much to their parents to know the truth. He resented his youngest brother for having made him promise to keep the secret a while longer.

"Dad—do you ever wonder what it would be like if Kyle suddenly showed up, all grown-up?" he couldn't help asking, knowing he was skirting a dangerous line.

Lou's fingers tightened for a moment on Ethan's shoulder, and then he dropped his hand to his side. "I can't tell you how many times I've imagined that happening. It's haunted both me and your mother all these years that we never found Kyle's body to bury properly. Made it harder to believe he was really dead."

He ran a hand over his thin brown hair, looking momentarily older than his sixty-five years. "I looked for him every day for a full year after he disappeared. I kept hoping maybe someone found him alive downstream and took him to a foster home or something. He was just a toddler, after all. He couldn't really tell anyone who he was or how to contact his family. But with all the publicity that surrounded his disappearance, it would be highly unlikely that the authorities and the child welfare system wouldn't have contacted us if a toddler boy had been found."

"But what if it did happen? He'd be a stranger to us. To you and Mom. He'd have led a whole life that didn't include us. Would that be more painful to you and Mom than finally having let him go?"

"What's bringing this up, Ethan? Why are you asking these questions?"

Ethan wished now that he'd kept his mouth shut. His father

was not a stupid man. Fortunately, no one had told him yet about Aislinn's special "gifts"—Ethan and Aislinn had decided to wait for the proper time to break that little tidbit to his parents—or Lou would be rapidly putting two and two together.

"I guess it's just that anniversary you mentioned earlier," he said brusquely, picking up his coffee cup again. "I couldn't help thinking about it. Why don't we go see if there's a baseball game on TV? I'll have to head back home soon, got some paperwork to do for tomorrow."

His dad's voice stopped him as he headed for the kitchen doorway. "Ethan."

"Yes?"

"In answer to your question, no. It wouldn't be more painful to us if Kyle were somehow miraculously returned to us now. No matter what sort of life he'd led, no matter what he would be like now, he would still be our son, and we would love him. I'm sure I speak for both of us when I say that we would give almost everything we have just for the chance to see him again. We never got a chance to say goodbye, you know."

Ethan swallowed hard. "Let's go watch a game," he said gruffly after a moment.

He walked wearily into his own house a little over an hour later. His phone started ringing as soon as he stepped inside. He didn't have to check the caller ID to know who it was. "H'lo."

"Are you okay?" His fiancée's voice sounded concerned.

"I'm okay. Just had dinner with my parents."

"Oh." That seemed to be explanation enough for her. "I had a feeling that something was troubling you, and that I should call you. Was it a difficult evening?"

He was no longer surprised, of course, that she knew when he was troubled. It didn't even bother him so much now to know that they would always share that intimate bond. "It was… awkward. Dad brought up Kyle. Fortunately, Mom wasn't in the room then."

"It must have been very hard for you not to tell your father about Mark."

"Oh, yeah. As it was, I almost said more than I should have. Mark really shouldn't have asked me to make that promise."

"But you'll keep your word. You are an honorable man."

He smiled, already feeling better. "Now you're just trying to flatter me into a good mood."

"Perhaps. But it also happens to be a fact."

"Yeah, well, you're biased. Because you love me." He had to say that aloud every so often just to remind himself that it was true.

"Also a fact." She waited a beat, then said, "Why don't you call him, Ethan?"

"Call who?"

"You know who I mean. Mark. You should call him."

"I'm not so sure he'd want to hear from me. He seemed pretty relieved when we left."

"He was overwhelmed. The two of you can never be close unless one of you reaches out."

"And you think I should be the one."

"Well, you are the older one."

He was getting kind of tired of being reminded of his age tonight. He was still three and a half years away from forty, for crying out loud. "Maybe I'll give him a call tomorrow. See if he has the results from the DNA test yet."

"He hasn't. But I think you should call him tonight. It isn't all that late. And I have a feeling he'd like to hear from you tonight."

Who was he to argue with Aislinn's feelings? "Maybe I will. I wish you were here, Aislinn."

"It won't be much longer," she promised. "I'll be there for the rest of our lives."

He smiled for the first time since he'd left his parents' house. "I'm going to hold you to that."

Mark was seriously in need of a morale boost Friday evening. He was tired after a long day of work, and discouraged because he and Rachel had barely had a moment alone together since she'd left his bed Wednesday. She didn't seem to be avoiding him, exactly. He didn't see second thoughts in her eyes when they were together. It was just that her schedule was so hectic, so controlled by other people that there was almost no time left for herself. Or for him.

Moping around his house like a lovesick schoolboy, he thought about going out to a bar or to the gym or something. It wasn't all that late yet. He was too young to spend a Friday night in front of the TV, too old to spend it daydreaming about the girl of his dreams. He could always call a friend and arrange to do something more interesting.

The problem was, he wasn't really in the mood to call anyone but Rachel. And that, he thought in exasperation, was just pathetic.

When the phone rang, he picked it up eagerly, thinking maybe she'd gotten through with her schedule early that evening. Maybe he could talk her into coming over for a nightcap. Or maybe for a little more. "Hello?"

"Mark, it's Ethan."

He tried to conceal his disappointment. "How's it going?"

"Not bad. You?"

"Fine."

"Er, Aislinn seemed to think you might need cheering up this evening."

"Did she." He was going to have to get used to having a psychic sister-in-law. "And she thought you'd be the one to do that?"

"Apparently. So…are you okay?"

The call seemed as awkward for Ethan as it felt to Mark. He wondered why Ethan had made the effort, since it didn't seem to be in his nature to reach out quite this way. Was it only because Aislinn had told him to? "I'm fine, really. But thanks for asking."

"I don't suppose you've heard anything about the tests."

"No, not yet. I promised I'd let you know as soon as I get the results. I could hear by Monday."

"Right. So, how's work going? Have you started your new partnership yet?"

"Yes. This week. I'm settling in, getting to know everyone at the clinic, seeing patients. Started hospital rounds this morning. Within a couple of weeks, I'll be fully into the routine, working my usual ten-to-twelve-hour days."

"Sounds like a tough schedule."

"I guess. But there's nothing else I'd rather be doing."

"You sound like Joel. He's either working or on call just about all the time, but he loves taking care of sick kids."

It really was odd that both Mark and Joel had gone into medicine, even though they had been raised so differently. Maybe at least that would give Mark something to talk about with his middle brother when they finally met. "And do you feel that way about business consulting?"

"Yeah, I guess. I prefer being my own boss, setting my own hours. I never would have made it in medicine. I don't like people that much."

Mark laughed a little in response to Ethan's drawled remark, but he didn't completely buy it. Ethan had to be pretty good with people or he wouldn't be successful at consulting with small business owners. In a way, he took care of struggling businesses the way his brothers dealt with physical ailments. But because that seemed a little fanciful, he didn't say it out loud.

"How's your decorating going?" Ethan asked. "Got your house finished yet?"

"No, we've got a few weeks to go yet. Takes a while to get all the ordered furniture in."

"Yeah, that's why I tend to buy right off the sales floor. I'm not into deferred gratification."

"I'm not, either," Mark admitted ruefully. "I'd like to have had it all done in a couple of days so I wouldn't have to bother with it all for longer than that, but Rachel talked me into doing it 'right.' At least, a decorator's version of 'right.' As it is, she says we're moving pretty fast considering we're doing a whole house."

"How is Rachel?"

Sensing that Ethan was really asking if Mark was still seeing Rachel beyond work, he replied, "She's fine. Very busy. And Aislinn?"

"The same. Trying to get ready to move here. I'll tell you, I'm looking forward to having her here all the time. This long-distance romance stuff sucks."

Mark laughed again, but his amusement was wry. He identified all too well with Ethan's frustration—and he and Rachel were at least living in the same state.

Though she had a key, Rachel rang the bell when she arrived at Mark's house Saturday morning. He opened the door to her with a smile.

Her heart tripped, as it always did when she saw him. He was dressed for a casual day in jeans and a perfectly fitted green polo shirt that made his eyes look like jade. She had dressed for comfort herself, in a scoop-neck yellow T-shirt, a full, printed cotton skirt that fell softly to below her knees, and a pair of yellow leather flip-flops. "Good morning."

"Good morning." He moved out of the way to let her inside. "You look nice."

"Thank you." She heard the door close behind her, and she looked over her shoulder with a smile. "So where would you like to start?"

"I was thinking my bedroom."

Her smile deepened. "But we've already finished in your bedroom."

His grin turned wicked, and her knees almost melted. "Sweetheart, we aren't anywhere near finished in my bedroom," he said. And while she was still laughing, he tugged her into his arms.

Chapter Ten

Mark lay on his left side, propped on one arm, his head cradled in his hand. The drapes were drawn, so the room was in shadow except for the light that spilled in from the open doorway. Still, Rachel could see that he was smiling as she lay against the pillows looking up at him.

He reached out with his free hand to twist a strand of her hair around his finger. "I'm glad you were able to get some time off this morning."

"I try not to work every weekend. Although, I was thinking that we could maybe do a little shopping this afternoon. There's a really nice antique mall on Cheshire Bridge Road and I think you might find a few things you like for your den and office."

He chuckled. "Even when you take a day off, you're working."

She couldn't help laughing at herself. "I know. But I have to confess, shopping for accessories doesn't feel like work to me. I honestly love it."

"It's nice that you enjoy your work so much. That you can

make a living doing what you love to do. I feel pretty much the same way about my career. That is, when I'm not having to deal with paperwork and insurance regulations and government bureaucracy and the other entanglements that go along with practicing medicine these days. But actually getting to take care of patients makes the rest of it tolerable, for me, at least."

"I'm not crazy about the paperwork, either. Or the tax and payroll stuff. And don't even get me started on insurance. I've also got to deal with all the usual concerns of running a new small business. So many fail in the first couple of years that it makes me rather paranoid about mine. I try to keep expenses in check and do as much promotion as I can afford and encourage referrals from my clients, but it's still a job-to-job business. Not exactly a secure, steady income yet, though I am paying my rent and my bills."

"It took a lot of courage for you to go out on your own so young."

She shrugged. "It sort of evolved that way. While Robbie and I were married, I worked as a design consultant for a large furniture store to support us while he got his restaurant established. I started getting freelance decorating jobs during that time, and I loved them. Then, after the divorce, I used the money he paid me for my share of the restaurant to open my own business. It was scary, but something I really needed to try. I figured the worst that would happen was that I'd have to close shop and work for someone else again, but so far it's going pretty well. Maybe I should pay your brother to look over my operation and make sure I'm set up for long-term success."

She felt him stiffen a little in response to her reference to Ethan. "I'm sure you're going to be fine," he said. "You seem to know what you're doing."

It occurred to her that this wasn't exactly the most romantic conversation to be having in his bed. What were they doing talking business when they had so little time alone together? And he certainly didn't want to talk about his family.

She reached up to wrap a hand around his neck. "I know

exactly what I'm doing," she assured him, and pulled his mouth down to hers.

He smiled against her lips, easing himself down on top of her, gathering her into his arms. She pushed against his shoulder and rolled him beneath her. Straddling him, she caught his hands and held them by the wrists above his head.

"I think it's going to be a while before we get around to that shopping trip," she murmured, her hair falling around her face as she gazed down at him.

His smile was a little shaky now, his voice rough when he replied, "I'm not in any hurry."

"That's good." She lowered her head to nip at his lower lip. "This may take some time…"

It was more than an hour later when Rachel and Mark finally left the bedroom, fully dressed and on their way out to have lunch and do some shopping. They had made it almost to his front door when Rachel's cell phone rang.

Mark exhaled gustily. "Don't you ever turn that thing off?"

It was the closest he'd ever come to sounding snappish with her. Rachel gave him a look and reached for the phone. "I can't just turn it off. There could be an emergency."

"I know. Sorry." He turned away to give her a semblance of privacy for the call.

"Hello?"

"Rachel? It's Dani. Can you come over?"

"Has something happened? Is something wrong?"

"No. I just want to see you today."

Relieved, Rachel glanced at Mark's back. "I'm afraid I can't right now."

"Then can I come to your place? I really need to talk."

Her sister sounded distressed—but then she always sounded distressed lately. "I'd be happy to talk to you, but can it wait? I'm busy with something else right now."

"Are you with *him?* Dr. Wonderful?"

The rather snide tone made Rachel's defenses go up. "Look, Dani, I—"

"I'm sorry," her sister cut in meekly. "I was just hoping you could make time for me today. I really need to talk to you, Ray-Ray."

Rachel folded, as she always did. "I'll call you later, okay? Maybe we can get together this evening. Why don't I buy you dinner?"

"I—" Dani hesitated, then said, "I don't know. Kurt might want to do something tonight."

"You don't know yet?"

"He said he would try to call me later."

"So you're going to sit by the phone all day in case he decides to call you?"

Now Dani was the one who sounded defensive. "I'm not sitting by the phone. I have my cell."

"Oh, right. That's so much different."

"If you're going to be snotty, I might as well hang up."

"I'm not trying to be—" She stopped herself with a sigh. "Look, I'll call you later this afternoon, okay? We'll try to get together."

"Okay," Dani agreed glumly. "Later."

She disconnected without a goodbye.

Rachel turned to Mark. "Sorry. We can go now."

"Look, I didn't mean to be insensitive earlier. If you need to go be with your sister, we can shop another time."

Though she still felt a little guilty for turning Dani down, something she did so very rarely, Rachel shook her head. "She just wants to complain about her boyfriend and our mother again. I can listen to that later. You and I don't have many opportunities to get your shopping done, especially now that you're back at work."

"You're sure?" he asked, looking as though he felt obligated to make certain.

"I'm sure." She tucked her purse beneath her arm. "Let's go."

* * *

He could watch Rachel shop for hours. And what did that say about how far gone he was over her?

Wearing an indulgent smile, he followed her through an import store they'd gone to after leaving their second antiques mall of the day. She seemed utterly fascinated by a display of beaded runners in sheer, jewel-toned fabrics.

"These are great," she murmured, running a hand over the cloth in a rather sensuous way that made his throat tighten. "Totally wrong for your place, but great."

"Maybe we could make one work?" he asked, watching her hand.

She smiled and shook her head, turning away. "No. I know these are too fussy and feminine for your taste. You don't need one, anyway."

Sheets, he thought. Maybe they should be shopping for sheets. He had several sets of those, too, but he wouldn't mind watching Rachel stroking the fabric.

"Look at these carved teak animals," she said, drawing him across the aisle by his hand. "They're pretty cool, aren't they?"

"Yeah. Cool."

Looking up at him, she shook her head. "You aren't looking at the animals."

"No," he admitted, turning to rest his forearms on her shoulders. "I guess I'm not."

Ignoring their surroundings, she spread her hands on his chest. "You're tired of shopping, aren't you? I can't blame you. Most guys would have bailed a long time ago."

He bent his head to brush a kiss across the tip of her nose. "I'm not most guys. And I'm not tired of shopping. I'm just going through withdrawal. I think it's been at least an hour since I kissed you."

Smiling, she rose on tiptoes to press her lips briefly to his.

"Will that hold you until we leave this store?" she asked, lowering herself back down.

"I don't know. There's a display of futon beds in the back…"

She laughed and stepped away from him. "Forget it."

He sighed dramatically. "I suppose the kiss will have to hold me."

Nodding congenially toward a gawking teenage salesgirl, Rachel directed his attention to the carvings again. He dragged his attention away from her long enough to select an elephant with an imperiously lifted trunk and a leopard in full-stalk mode. Approving his choices, Rachel assured him that she could find the perfect place for them in his home.

He carried the bag out to his car and added it to the packages they had already piled in the backseat. Closing the door, he turned to Rachel, who stood behind him. "I'm not sure it's going to hold much more."

She grasped the handle of the passenger door. "I think we've done enough shopping for today, anyway."

He'd reached out at the same time she did to open the door, his hand landing on top of hers. He stood just behind her, his arm wrapped around her to reach the door. He was having a hard time making himself want to move away.

She looked up at him, and the amusement faded from her face in response to whatever she saw in his expression. Her eyes darkened to a deep charcoal blue and her lips parted just a little, drawing his gaze to them. Once again forgetting that there was anyone in the area but them, he dipped his head toward hers.

"Rachel? Is that you?"

Mark and Rachel turned simultaneously in response to the shrill question. A well-rounded young woman with streaky blond hair and thick-lashed blue eyes crossed the parking lot toward them, followed by an average-looking guy with thinning hair and what appeared to be a permanent furrow on his high forehead.

Rachel made a low sound, and somehow Mark knew before she spoke who the other couple was. She moved her hand from beneath his, but she didn't move away from him when she said, "Hello, Kaylee. Robbie. This is a surprise."

Mark was subjected to two intense inspections, avid curiosity from the woman and cool suspicion from the man. Taking the hint, Rachel introduced them briefly, "Mark Thomas, Kaylee and Robbie Blankenship."

"Nice to meet you both," he said politely, nodding in lieu of offering his right hand, which was still resting on the door handle.

"It's nice to meet you, too," Kaylee assured him. "We heard Rachel was dating someone new. You *are* the doctor, aren't you?"

He couldn't look at Rachel just then for fear that he would laugh. "Yes, I am."

"So what are y'all doing? Out shopping?"

"Yes, Rachel's helping me decorate my house."

"Really?" Kaylee glanced at Rachel. "I like to decorate my own home, but I suppose a busy doctor doesn't have time for things like that."

"I'd rather defer to Rachel's excellent taste than to live in the mess I would probably end up with on my own."

"Did you and Rachel start seeing each other before or after you hired her?" Robbie asked, and somehow the question sounded rather shady, coming from him.

"Listen, it was nice seeing you, but we have to run," Rachel said before Mark could reply. She glanced up at Mark, and following her unspoken suggestion, he opened the car door for her.

"I'll call you later, okay, Rach?" Robbie said, practically leaning into the car after she slid into the seat. "I've got a couple of things I need to discuss with you."

She nodded. "Yes, fine."

Mark closed the door between them. Robbie jumped back just in time to avoid having his hand closed in the door frame—or at least, he seemed to think it had been a close call, though Mark had been very deliberate in his timing.

Nodding toward the couple, he moved around the front of the

car. "Nice to meet you both," he said as he opened the driver's door. "Goodbye."

"Well, that was awkward," he said after buckling in and starting the car. He drove out of the parking lot, leaving the Blankenships looking after them.

"A bit," Rachel agreed, adjusting her seat belt across her bright cotton skirt.

"Any reason why your ex-husband hates my guts?"

A sideways glance revealed that Rachel looked startled by his question. "Robbie doesn't hate you. He doesn't even know you."

"Mmm." That wasn't the impression Mark had gotten. "So, what's his problem? He doesn't want you seeing anyone else, even though he's remarried, himself?"

"No," she said a little too forcefully. "That's not the case, at all. I think you just misread him."

"Yeah, maybe I did." But he hadn't.

Shaking his head, he focused on the road ahead, wondering how any man in his right mind could let Rachel slip away. How Robbie could have preferred Kaylee—or anyone, for that matter.

"Do you think you'll hear about the DNA tests Monday? I doubt that the lab is open today, on a Saturday."

He knew her change of subject had been deliberate, and that she had just as intentionally chosen a topic that would make him as uncomfortable as talking about her ex-husband made her. Well played, he acknowledged, even as he replied, "No, the lab isn't open today. I'll probably hear something early next week."

"I'm surprised Ethan hasn't called to ask if you'd heard."

"Actually, he called last night."

She turned in her seat to face him. "Ethan called you last night? You didn't mention it."

"No. It must have slipped my mind."

Her momentary silence told him she didn't really buy that careless explanation. "Did you have a nice chat?" she asked after a moment.

"I guess. He said to tell you hello."

"That was nice of him."

"He and Aislinn both enjoyed meeting you. I could tell they liked you."

"I liked them, too. Aislinn is a fascinating woman. I'm still not sure I entirely buy that she's psychic, but there is something different about her."

"Yeah, that's pretty much the way I feel about her. Ethan's obviously nuts about her."

"Did you and he talk for long?"

"Twenty minutes, maybe. We talked about our jobs and fishing—you know, our favorite gear and flies, that sort of thing."

"Did you talk about the family? Your parents?"

"No, not really. He said everyone was okay there."

It had been his choice not to ask many questions about the family, and Ethan hadn't volunteered much, perhaps following Mark's lead.

"So, how did it feel to talk to him? Are you starting to think of him as your brother?"

"I know him only marginally better than you do," he pointed out, his hands tightening for a moment on the steering wheel. "Right now, he's just a new acquaintance."

How he wished it were that simple.

"And you don't want to talk about it," Rachel said with a sigh.

He shrugged. "Not much to say at this point."

"Isn't there?" After a moment of silence, she straightened in her seat again. "We can pile all these things in one of the spare bedrooms when we get to your house, and I'll bring them out as I find places for them. I'll do a little more shopping on my own while you work next week. I can bring artwork and rugs to your house and you can choose which ones you like. I'll return the things you don't want to keep."

"Yeah, that'll work." He had the sense that he had disappointed her somehow, but he wasn't sure how. Because he didn't want to talk about his newfound family right now? As he had pointed out, there just wasn't much to say. He hadn't even met them yet. How the hell was he supposed to know how he felt about them?

Her phone rang just as he drove into his garage. She answered it without even bothering to give him an apologetic look this time. "What is it, Dani?"

Though he couldn't make out the words, Mark could hear her sister's voice coming through the phone. It sounded as if she might be crying. He suspected that Rachel would be leaving very shortly.

He had just turned off the engine when she snapped her phone closed and confirmed his prediction. "I have to go."

He nodded without speaking.

"I'll help you carry these things inside first."

He reached for his door handle. "That's not necessary. I can get them. Go to your sister."

Climbing out of her seat, she looked at him over the top of the car. "I wouldn't go if she didn't need me."

"I know. I hope you can help her."

Still hesitating, she said, "You're sure you don't need help? We bought quite a few things."

He rounded the back of the car, wrapped a hand around the back of her neck and pressed a hard kiss on her mouth. "Go," he said when he released her. "Take care of your family."

Moistening her lips, she nodded, pulled her keys out of her purse and walked away from him.

Mark waited until she was gone before he turned to open the back door of his car. He paused with his hand on the handle, lowering his head to the top of the car for a moment, half considering pounding his forehead against the metal. And then he straightened and opened the door, reaching inside for the first package.

Chapter Eleven

Rachel thought—hoped—Mark might call her Sunday, just to talk, if nothing else. He didn't.

She didn't wait for his call, exactly. She went about her usual routine, attending church with her mother and grandmother, lunching with them afterward, eventually escaping to hole up in her apartment and work on a presentation for a new potential client, a lawyer who had purchased a home on the historic registry and was considering restoring it to turn-of-the-twentieth-century condition. But she thought about Mark. A lot.

She couldn't say exactly what the state of their budding relationship was at the moment. Though the day had started perfectly yesterday, it had ended a bit tensely. He had tried to hide it, but Mark had obviously been a little annoyed that she'd had to rush out on him again to tend to a member of her family. And if she were honest, she had to admit that she'd been a little miffed with him, too, for continuing to brush her off whenever she tried to ask about his feelings about the Brannon family.

Everything he had learned about his biological family, the entire prospect of being reunited with them again, had to be an intensely emotional development for Mark. And yet he continued to act as though he was pretty much unaffected by it all, at least in front of her.

If he was doing the same thing when she wasn't around—well, that didn't seem particularly healthy to her. And if he wasn't, if he was deliberately choosing not to discuss something so personal with her—then what did that mean? That the only relationship he was interested in with her was a physical one? She hadn't gotten that impression from him, but maybe she'd been wrong. If so, she'd like to know now so she didn't let herself start hoping for something more.

When the phone rang late Sunday evening, she practically snatched it up. She told herself she wasn't disappointed when she saw her friend Kristy's number on the ID screen. She hadn't talked to Kristy in a while, and it would be nice to catch up, she thought.

They talked for almost an hour, chatting about inconsequential things and telling one another what had been going on in their lives. Though Rachel talked about Mark's decorating job, one of her two biggest projects at the moment, she didn't tell her everything. And that felt strange because she and Kristy had always shared information like that.

After she hung up, she wondered why she hadn't told her friend that she was seeing Mark on a personal basis, as well as professional. She never came up with a conclusive answer, but she decided finally that maybe it was because she was still too conflicted about Mark to talk about him yet. Even to her longtime friend.

Maybe, she mused, that was exactly the way he felt about his family.

Mark's smile was weary when he arrived home from the clinic at just after 6:00 p.m. Monday. He walked the three steps down into the gathering room as Rachel was arranging red throw pillows on his new dusty-blue sectional sofa. Soft music greeted him, as she'd been testing the discreetly hidden music system and concealed speakers that also worked with the large, flat-screen TV installed over the fireplace.

"Wow," he said, looking around the room. "This is amazing. How did you get it all done in one day?"

"I had a lot of help today. Work had to stop on the Perkins job because of a gas leak, so I brought some of the crew in here. We've got your guest rooms started, too. Those rooms won't take long, since we bought all the furnishings off the sales floors."

He shrugged. "I figured I might need guest rooms soon, if…well, you know."

If his family came to visit him, she completed in her head. The thought had already occurred to her, actually. Which meant she had spent a little extra time working to make the quickly furnished rooms look especially nice.

Running a hand along the back of the sofa, he looked at her. "Is everyone else gone now?"

"Yes. I stayed to do a few last-minute things. And—I wanted to see you."

He reached up to loosen the red-patterned tie he wore with dark slacks and a soft blue shirt that looked amazing against his tanned skin. "Anything in particular?"

"No. I just wanted to see you."

The muscles in his face seemed to relax a little in response to that. Had he been expecting something different? "I'm glad," he said, coming to a stop in front of her.

She placed her hands on his chest. "You look tired. Rough day?"

Shrugging, he replied, "Yeah, a little. Sounds like yours was, too. How big a deal is the gas leak?"

"Not too. We'll be able to get back in tomorrow. I'll need to spend a few hours over there tomorrow morning, but I can work in your dining room tomorrow afternoon."

Resting his hands on her hips, he pulled her closer. "I'm not on any deadline, you know. You can take your time."

"I know. But I also know how impatient you are to have everything finished."

"Oh, I don't know." He raised a hand to cup her cheek. "Not if it means seeing you less."

Relieved that the tension that had gripped them last time they'd parted seemed to have eased, for now at least, she reached up to place her hand over his. "I think we can work something out in that respect."

Sliding his hand to the back of her head, his fingers tangling in her hair, he lifted her face to his. "Good."

The kiss started out gentle, his lips pressing lightly, moving softly. He nipped at her lower lip, pulling it lightly between his teeth, then running the tip of his tongue over it as if to soothe the nonexistent marks he'd left behind. She ran her hands behind his back to clutch at his broad shoulders, her head falling back as her muscles relaxed. He took advantage of the opportunity to lower his mouth, nibbling at the skin below her jaw, behind her ear.

She murmured her pleasure at the sensations he aroused in her. Flexing her fingers into his muscles, she rubbed her leg against his in one long, lazy stroke that made him groan into her throat. He kissed her again, his tongue dipping between her lips to tangle teasingly with hers.

From those cleverly hidden speakers, Ronan Keating began to croon, "When You Say Nothing At All," and even though it was a total cliché, Rachel felt her knees weaken. Still kissing her, Mark swayed in a stationary dance. And she felt herself losing yet another part of her heart to him.

With a strangled sound escaping her, she wrapped her arms around his neck, pressing herself more intimately against him. Those gentle, playful kisses changed, becoming hard, hungry, deep. And neither one of them even tried to hide the strength of their reactions.

Drawing a long, shuddering breath, Mark finally released her mouth, resting his forehead against hers as they took a moment to recover. "I think I need to sit down."

Opening her eyes, she smiled up at him. "How fortunate that you have furniture in here now."

"Yeah." Pressing one last, light kiss against her forehead, he put a few inches between them and drew her to the big, sectional sofa. "Oh, yeah. This is as comfortable as I remember," he said a moment later, sitting against the cushions with one arm around her shoulders.

Nestling into his side, Rachel let her shoes slip off her feet and drew her legs up beside her. "So, you like the room?" she asked, needing to ground herself in casual conversation.

Blinking a little, as if to clear his vision, he took a moment to look around. The L-shaped blue sectional, piled with colorful red, cream and smoky-blue throw pillows, faced the big fireplace and TV screen. A Turkish rug with a dark red background and blue-and-tan figuring provided warmth to the wood floor. In lieu of a traditional coffee table, he and Rachel had found a large, flat-topped storage chest finished in an espresso stain, which was also the finish on the end table on his right and the console table behind the sofa. Two comfortable swivel rockers were placed to allow conversation with anyone sitting on the couch and also to view the TV screen.

In a corner behind them was a fully stocked wet bar with a dark granite countertop and a beveled-edge mirror above. The octagonal game table sat in the corner to the left of the fireplace, surrounded by the four comfortable leather-seated chairs he had selected. On the wall to the right of the fireplace two sets of French doors led out to the stone terrace that was also accessible from the breakfast room.

Rachel had decorated the tables and built-in bookcases with some of the items she and Mark had picked up on their shopping outings, mixing in the few personal items he'd had in a box upstairs. A couple of big seashells. A chess set with an intricately patterned wooden board and finely carved wooden pieces, one side ebony, the other a pale boxwood. An antique brass clock.

It made her sad that there were no photographs he wanted to display. It was almost as if he was trying to forget his past had ever existed prior to moving into this house. She knew he'd been a happy man when she'd first met him, before he'd heard about his true beginnings. They'd even talked about his childhood with his rather reclusive, single mother on that first pleasant dinner date. He'd said it had been a bit lonely, but otherwise satisfying.

Whatever mementos he had of that childhood were hidden away somewhere now, and she wondered if he ever intended to look at them again.

"It's a great room," he approved after his inspection. "Can't wait to have the guys over for poker."

She was glad he looked forward to entertaining here, but she suspected his family would be his first guests. Resting her head on his shoulder, she asked, "Did you hear from the DNA test today?"

Just as she'd half expected, he stiffened a little before answering, "No. I guess the lab's backed up. Lots of paternity cases in front of us, I suppose."

He changed the subject before she could respond. "How's your sister? Have you been able to talk any sense into her?"

"Oh, I don't know." She sighed heavily. "Mother's right, I think. Dani's determined to make things work out with Kurt just to prove to everyone that they were wrong and she was right about him. He's making her miserable, but she continues to defend him and she gets angry and defensive when anyone tries to point out the truth."

"Then why does she want you to keep coming to talk to her, if she isn't going to listen?"

"I think she believes I'll come around to her side if she can just convince me that I've misjudged him. Maybe she secretly hopes I'll convince her otherwise, but if so I haven't succeeded yet."

He rested his cheek on her hair. "Your family certainly does expect a lot of you."

"No more than any family, I guess."

He was silent for a moment, and she regretted the way she'd phrased her answer. Since he'd grown up without his family, and had been on his own for so long, he could be forgiven for not understanding the demands and responsibilities that were all part of the deal.

Was he suddenly wondering if his newfound family would place as many demands on him as her clan did on her?

"Any of my family would be there for me, just as I am for them," she assured him.

He murmured something that might have been intended as a noncommittal response. Did he doubt that she would have the same support she gave if she needed it? While it was true that she very rarely asked for anything from her family, or from anyone else, for that matter, she took comfort in knowing that they were there for her.

Maybe all this talk of family was edging a bit too close to the sore spots between them for Mark's peace of mind. He slid his hand up her arm to tilt her chin up toward him and dropped a light kiss on her lips. "Do you have plans for this evening?"

"No, as it happens, I'm free." Unless her phone rang, calling her away for some sort of family problem, she thought. Though she kept it to herself, she was pretty sure she saw the same thought mirrored in Mark's eyes.

Still, he kept his tone light when he asked, "Will you stay awhile?"

Wrapping her arm around his neck, she murmured against his lips, "I would love to."

They cooked together, scavenging in Mark's kitchen to find chicken breasts and fresh vegetables. Clipping some herbs from his new mini herb garden, Rachel cooked the chicken while he nuked sweet potatoes and steamed broccoli florets. They talked the whole time they worked, chattering about nothing of any consequence, but learning even more about each other in the process.

Being with him made her happy, she realized as they lingered over the meal, sitting at the kitchen table and sipping wine by candlelight. It was as simple—and as complicated—as that. She was beginning to worry that the reverse would be true, also. She'd been quite content on her own for the past three years. She couldn't help being a bit concerned that he had the power to change that.

When they'd finally stretched out the meal as long as they could, they cleaned the kitchen, which took longer than it should have because Mark kept stopping to kiss her or nibble the back of her neck. None of which she minded, of course, but it did distract her from what she'd been doing.

While he put the last item in the dishwasher and closed the door, she wiped the counters, then rinsed the towel she had used and draped it over the sink divider to dry. She turned, only to find herself crowded backward against the granite countertop when Mark's arms went around her and he loomed over her.

"So," he said, smiling down at her, "what would you like to do now?"

She walked her fingers up his chest to rest her hands on his shoulders. "What did you have in mind?"

"We could crash on my new couch and watch my new TV."

She laughed. "Yes, we could do that."

"And maybe later…" He nuzzled her cheek.

She tilted her face for him. "Mmm?"

"Ice cream."

"You're a wicked man, Mark Thomas."

"So I've been told."

He kissed her very thoroughly, then stepped back, leaving her wanting more. "Want a soda or anything?"

"No, I'm fine, thank you," she said, though her voice sounded a bit shaky to her own ears.

"I'm just going to check my mailbox and I'll join you in the den, okay?"

She slid a hand down his cheek as she moved past him. "Don't be long," she murmured, pleased when his smile faltered for a moment.

He cleared his throat. "I won't be."

True to his word, he joined her in the den only minutes later. She had already settled onto the sofa with the remote. She looked up as Mark strolled into the room. He'd lost the tie a long time ago, and had opened the top button of his blue shirt and rolled the sleeves back on his forearms. And she completely lost interest in whatever was playing on the television screen.

He carried a stack of envelopes, which he shuffled through as he walked. "Bills," he muttered, giving her a wry smile, "I've lived here barely a month, and I'm already getting the…"

His voice faded as he stopped to stare down at the return address on one of the envelopes.

After a moment, Rachel asked, "Mark? Is everything okay?"

Setting the rest of his mail on the sofa table, he sank onto the couch beside her, still looking down at the envelope that had caught his attention. "It's from the DNA lab."

"Oh." She set the remote aside and sat up straighter. "Your results?"

"Yeah. I guess." But still he didn't open it.

"Don't you want to see the results?" she prodded gently.

He looked at her, and the look on his face made her heart twist. "I don't know."

She laid a hand on his thigh, giving him a little squeeze of support.

Inhaling a deep breath, he turned the envelope over and opened the flap, drawing out a single sheet of paper. He scanned the fine print on it quickly.

She bit her lower lip as he looked up at her.

"The DNA evidence indicates strongly that Ethan and I are brothers," he said. "That's about as conclusive as it gets in science talk."

She nodded. "That's pretty much what you expected, isn't it? That Ethan's story would be confirmed?"

"Yeah."

So why did he still look as though he hadn't been fully prepared to hear the answer? "Are you okay?"

Whether by intention or accident, his eyes were suddenly shuttered, his expression impossible to read. "I'm fine. Like you said, this is what I expected to hear."

He had shut her out so quickly. It hurt, but she tried to push her own bruised feelings aside, reminding herself that he was going through a tough time. "Are you going to call Ethan now?"

"I—yeah." He sounded predictably reluctant. "I told him I would let him know as soon as I heard something."

"Do you want me to leave?"

"No. I'd rather you'd stay, unless you need to go."

The speed with which he had replied—almost before she'd completed the sentence—reassured her that he wasn't pushing her aside completely. He just wasn't ready to talk about his innermost feelings of betrayal and confusion, hurt and uncertainty. That was understandable, she told herself. She could be patient. "I can stay a while longer."

He made an attempt at a smile and cupped her face with his left hand. Covering his hand with her own, she nestled her cheek into his warm palm, her other hand still resting on his thigh. Mark leaned his head down to kiss her, softly, lingeringly, and then he drew a long, hard breath and moved back. "I guess I'll call Ethan now."

She nodded, reaching up almost subconsciously to touch her face where his hand had been.

Pulling a card out of his wallet, Mark opened his cell phone and dialed the number written on the card. "Ethan? It's Mark. The test results are in."

Despite his invitation for her to stay, Rachel gave him a semblance of privacy during the call by focusing on the television screen while he talked. One of the twenty-four-hour cable news channels was tuned in, and headlines ran across the bottom of the screen, but she had a hard time focusing on them. The only news she was interested in was taking place right here in this room, she thought, and then winced when she realized that the media would probably be fascinated by Mark's story if they should get wind of it. He would probably hate that—and she suspected that Ethan would absolutely abhor it.

His conversation didn't last long. She looked around at him when he snapped the phone shut and tossed it onto the coffee table chest with a weary gesture. "I don't suppose Ethan was surprised by the results, either," she said.

Pushing a hand through his hair, he shook his head. "He said he never had any doubt. And then he told me he was pleased to have official confirmation of his belief."

"When is he going to tell the rest of the family?"

"I'm not sure. I told him to do so whenever he thinks best."

"Are you going there?"

He shook his head firmly. "They can come here if they want to meet me. I can't leave right now. I've got the rest of the house to finish and I just started at the clinic."

His turf, she mused. That was where he wanted the first meeting to take place, giving him some very small sense of control. She supposed she couldn't blame him. So much of the situation he found himself in now had been orchestrated by other people.

"Maybe they won't even want to come," he added a bit tentatively. "After all, they don't know me. They've lived quite contentedly, apparently, for thirty years without me. Seems like it would just be more painful for them than anything."

She gave him a look. "You don't believe that. You know they'll want to meet you."

He sighed. "Yeah. I guess," he muttered.

"Surely you want to meet them, too. They're your family, Mark. Your parents. Your brothers. The fact that you've spent the past thirty years apart doesn't change that. It wasn't your fault, and it wasn't theirs. Maybe you can't ever get those years back, but you can make new memories together. You can have a family again."

"I've been getting along pretty well on my own, too."

"Yes, you have. But that doesn't mean there isn't room in your life for family."

"Seems to me like families are more trouble than they're worth sometimes."

That sounded like another dig at her own. "I told you my family is there for me as much as I am for them."

"Funny. I've known you for several weeks now and I've never seen you call them to take care of every little problem that crops up the way they do with you."

She took a deep breath, trying to hold on to her patience.

Mark reached out to take her hands in his. "I'm sorry. I don't mean to take my frustration out on you. You don't deserve that. You're only trying to help."

"I understand."

Looking suddenly annoyed again, he shook his head. "Don't let me off the hook that easily. Darn it, Rachel, this is why everyone expects so much from you. You keep letting them get away with it."

"Fine," she said a bit curtly. "I'll be irritated with you, instead."

His smile was rueful when he lifted her hands to his lips. "I don't want that, either," he confessed.

"What *do* you want, Mark?"

"You," he grated, pulling her into his arms. "All I want right now is you."

She lifted her face to his, offering him everything she had to give. Yet some deeply buried part of her mind wondered if Mark was giving as much as he seemed willing to take.

Chapter Twelve

Ethan faced a captive audience in his parents' living room late Tuesday afternoon. His parents sat in their favorite chairs, watching him expectantly. Joel and Nic sat side by side and hand in hand on the couch, both of them looking curious about why they'd been asked to take an unscheduled couple of days off from their jobs in Arkansas to come to Alabama.

Aislinn, who sat on Nic's other side, was the only one of them who knew why Ethan had called this family meeting. She smiled at him sympathetically, knowing better than anyone else how difficult this was for him.

Though he had assured everyone that this was not an emergency, and that he had good news, not bad, he could see anxiety in his mother's eyes as she looked up at him, her hands twisting in her lap. "Ethan? We're all here, just as you asked. Please tell us now what's so urgent before I go crazy with all these terrible possibilities in my head."

"It's nothing bad, Mom," he promised her. "I have some

news that I wanted to tell you all at once, since it involved the whole family."

"What news?" she asked, puzzled. And then she looked quickly at Aislinn, her eyes widening. "Oh, my goodness. Are the two of you expecting?"

"No," Ethan said quickly, while Aislinn laughed a bit self-consciously. "We'll wait until after the wedding to start thinking about that development, okay?"

Though she looked a bit disappointed, Elaine nodded. "Then what is it?"

He pushed his hands into his pockets and nodded toward a framed photograph on the mantel. "It's about the family," he repeated, then waited for a moment until everyone's eyes turned toward the photo. It was a studio shot of the Brannon clan more than thirty years earlier. Lou and Elaine, looking young and proud, Ethan and Joel spiffed up and restless as they tried to be still for the camera and baby Kyle grinning in his mother's lap.

"I've recently come into some information," he began, figuring he would give the details later. "It's about what happened the afternoon that Kyle disappeared."

Elaine raised a hand to her throat, as if it had tightened in response to the painful reminder.

Lou frowned. "What information?" he wanted to know. "Have you somehow found out where Carmen was going when she left the house that day?"

Because he was married to a police officer, Joel leaped to another possibility. "Have the, uh—" He glanced at his mother before finishing cautiously. "Have the remains been found?"

"Yes to your question, Dad. I'll get to yours in a minute, Joel."

Ethan had been as careful as he could in setting this up, but he had never been known for either patience or tact. He figured the best way to tell somebody something was just to say it. Quickly and without mincing words. "Carmen and Kyle didn't die in the flood that day. She pushed her car into the river to make it look as though they had died, and then she took off with Kyle to raise him as her own son."

A long, stunned silence followed his blunt announcement. Aislinn winced a little, as if she thought he might have been a little too brusque, but she nodded supportively at him, anyway. Nic glanced at her, and Aislinn nodded again to signify that she already knew everything Ethan was going to say.

"Ethan." Elaine's voice was little more than a whisper, her face pale and taut. Lou didn't seem able to speak at all. "This isn't funny."

He was more gentle with her than he would have been with anyone else who might have accused him of trying to make such a tasteless joke. "It's the truth, Mom. Kyle isn't dead. I've seen him. We were tested for DNA comparisons, and the evidence is overwhelming. He's alive, and living in Georgia."

"Oh, my God."

Joel was on his feet in an instant, kneeling by his mother's chair and taking her trembling hand in his. "You're absolutely certain of this, Ethan?" he asked unsteadily.

Meeting his brother's eyes without flinching, Ethan replied, "Completely."

"Oh, my God," Elaine said again, her eyes filling with tears. "Kyle."

Letting Joel tend to their mother, Ethan moved to rest his hand on his father's rigid shoulder. "He answers to the name Mark these days. Mark Thomas. It's the only name he remembers. The family resemblance is very strong. Aislinn says anyone could tell by looking at us that we're brothers. And, Joel, he's a doctor. He treats senior citizens in a family practice clinic near Atlanta."

"Why?" Lou asked, his voice raw. "Why would Carmen have done this to us? What possible reason could she have had for taking our son?"

"I guess we'll never know that, Dad," Ethan replied, his chest aching as he watched his family struggle with their emotions. "She's dead."

"Good," Nic said with typical ferocity. "Although I'd have enjoyed being the one to slap the cuffs on her."

"You've met him, too, Aislinn?" Joel asked, having processed everything Ethan had said.

She nodded. "Yes. I liked him very much. He seems like a good man."

Still holding his mother's hand, Joel straightened to his feet, giving Ethan a hard look. "When you were in Georgia a couple of weeks ago, supposedly on business, you were actually with Kyle?"

"He prefers Mark," Ethan reminded him. "And yes, Aislinn and I stayed a couple of days there, though we didn't spend that much time with him, actually."

"And you didn't tell us?" Joel looked angry now, his tumultuous emotions turning toward the one person he could lash out at. "You didn't think we would want to know the minute you did?"

"Mark asked Ethan not to say anything until the DNA results came back," Aislinn said, coming to Ethan's defense. "He wanted to make sure before everyone's hopes were raised. And I think he needed time to process what he'd learned about his past. He had just found out that everything he ever believed about himself was a lie. You can surely understand that it was a terrible blow for him."

Elaine was crying quietly into Joel's shoulder now. Lou stood and walked to the mantel, gazing at the photograph as if trying to picture the smiling toddler as a grown man. He asked over his shoulder, "Just how did you find him? How did you even know to look?"

Ethan turned to at Aislinn. "I think you should sit down again. There are a few more things you need to hear."

"Do not let go."

"I'm not letting go."

"Put your left hand right there. And the other here. Now, don't move."

Mark's voice was low and patient when he replied, "I'm not moving."

Rachel took a step backward. "Yes, that looks perfect. Now hold it while I get my pencil."

"You're going to have to hurry. This thing is heavy."

"Gripe, gripe, gripe." Crowding in beside him, she stood on tiptoes and placed a faint mark on the wall above the gilt frame of the still-life painting he held in place. "There. Now you can put it down and we'll set the nail."

He heaved an exaggerated sigh of relief when he set the painting carefully on the floor of the dining room. "Thank you."

She laughed and shook her head at him. "A studly guy like you ought to be able to hold something heavier than that painting."

He startled her by swooping on her, scooping her into his arms, and doing a quick spin, her feet dangling over his arm. She laughed and clutched his shoulders, breathless and delighted.

"Want to see me carry you up the stairs?" he asked.

Oh, yes. "Decorating now," she said, instead. "Stairs later."

"That does give me incentive," he conceded, planting a quick kiss on her lips before swinging her down to her feet.

It was Tuesday evening, and she'd stayed after her crews had left to spend a few hours alone with Mark. It had been Mark's idea to help her finish in the dining room, where she'd been working all afternoon arranging the traditional furniture beneath the gorgeous chandelier and hanging the elegant draperies that perfectly complemented the striking Oriental rug.

The house was shaping up nicely, and much more quickly than she had predicted. It wouldn't be long before the job was finished and she'd have no more excuses to hang around here. At least, none that were work related.

Mark had just hammered in the nail when Rachel's cell phone rang. Swallowing a groan, she actually considered ignoring it.

She couldn't even meet Mark's eyes when she lifted the phone to her ear.

"Rachel? Can you come? I—it's bleeding."

She stiffened. "Dani? Dani, what's wrong? What's bleeding?"

"Just come, okay?"

The line went dead. "Oh, my God."

Mark dropped the hammer. "What's wrong?"

"I don't know. It was Dani. Something's really wrong this time, Mark."

He took her arm. "I'll go with you."

"But I—"

He interrupted her firmly, "You said something about bleeding. You might need me."

She nodded to acknowledge the validity of that argument. And because her hands were shaking so hard, she asked, "Will you drive?"

He squeezed her arm. "Of course."

Following the directions Rachel gave him, Mark drove to Dani's apartment. He'd barely put the car into Park before Rachel was out of her seat, running toward her sister's door with Mark close behind her.

Dani opened the door to them, and Mark pushed past Rachel to catch Dani's arm. "Sit down," he said as she swayed. "Rachel, I need a wet washcloth, a cold pack or some ice in a plastic zip-close bag and some sort of antiseptic. Alcohol, hydrogen peroxide, whatever you can find. A first aid kit and a small flashlight would be helpful, as well."

"I don't—" Holding a trembling hand to her bruised face, Dani asked Rachel, "Why did you bring him?"

"Because she was with me when you called," Mark answered as Rachel hurried to retrieve the things he'd asked for. "And I'm a doctor. Which comes in handy occasionally. Like now."

As he'd spoken, he'd settled her on the couch, moved her hand out of the way and started to examine the bloody lump on the side of her face, just beside her left eye. He was relieved to see that it looked worse than it actually was. Though her face was covered with dried blood, the bleeding had stopped. She had a goose egg and the beginnings of a colorful bruise, but he saw no initial reason to be overly concerned.

Rachel appeared beside him, her arms loaded. "What do you need first?" she asked tightly. "Should I call an ambulance?"

"No," Dani and Mark said simultaneously.

"I don't need an ambulance," Dani insisted.

"It really isn't necessary," Mark agreed. "Though I'm reserving judgment on whether we should be calling the police."

"No," Dani said again, more forcefully this time. "You shouldn't have brought him, Rachel."

"Well, she did," he said with the frankness that served him well in his dealings with cantankerous seniors. "And since I'm here, I might as well tend to this cut. Rachel, did you find a flashlight?"

"Yes." She showed him a thin minilight and he noted in satisfaction that his matter-of-fact manner had calmed her enough to steady her hands. "Will this do?"

Giving her a quick smile, he said, "That will do perfectly, thank you. I'll go wash my hands and I'll be right back."

He wasn't gone long, and when he came back Dani was sobbing into Rachel's shoulder. She had already cried until her eyes were red and swollen, making it even harder for him to tell what was damage from the blow and what the result of her tears.

Extricating Dani from her sister, he tipped up her chin with one finger and flashed the light into her eyes, instructing her to follow the beam as he moved it, watching her pupils react as he aimed the light into them and away. Satisfied that she was responding normally, if rather sullenly, he turned off the light and handed it to Rachel, who waited silently nearby.

"I'm going to wash off the blood," he said, picking up the damp cloth. "I'll try not to be rough, but I need to see what's under it."

Dani nodded, refusing to look at him.

"Looks fist-shaped to me," he commented, as he stroked the cloth lightly over the swollen skin.

She said nothing.

"Will she need stitches?" Rachel wanted to know.

He studied the small split in the center of the swelling. "No, I don't think that will be necessary. It would be more likely to scar with stitches than without. Did you find bandages?"

She opened the first aid kit to display a good assortment of adhesive bandages, gauze and tape.

He set to work gently treating and dressing the cut, sensing that Dani was going to refuse any further treatment. He suspected that Rachel was just biding her time to start asking questions and that Dani was already framing answers in her head.

"That should do it," he said, setting the kit aside. "It looked worse than it was. Face and head wounds always bleed a lot. You're going to have a colorful bruise for a few days, but I doubt that you'll have a scar. Of course, if you want to make sure of that, you can see your own doctor, or even a plastic surgeon, though I think that would be an overreaction."

"You really think I'm that vain?" Dani asked him, almost in challenge.

"I don't know you well enough to gauge your level of vanity," he replied with a half smile and a light shrug. "Just giving you options."

Letting her dark hair fall over the bandage, she looked up at him through her lashes. "Thank you," she said, only a bit grudgingly.

"You're welcome. Now, do we call the police?"

Her expression turned stubborn again. "No."

"Dani—"

Looking up at her sister, Dani said, "I'm not calling the police, Rachel, so just let it go. It was mostly my fault, anyway."

Mark sighed. He'd heard this story before.

Dani looked at him defensively. "It was. I said some pretty harsh things. Anyone would have gotten mad."

"But not everyone would have responded with a swing," he replied. "Some people just leave when they get angry."

"He tried. I blocked the door. You see, a lot of it *was* my fault."

Mark leaned down so that he could look directly into her eyes. "It is never your fault when a man hits you," he said flatly. "I'm guessing he had the advantage of size and strength. He could have moved you out of the way without hurting you. I don't know if this is a pattern with him or something he did once and will never do again, but don't take the accountability away from him."

"You don't know him," she sniffled.

"No. But I've known other men who hit women, and it was always someone else's fault, according to them. You take away their personal responsibility and you remove any incentive for them to change their behavior."

"Has he ever hit you before?" Rachel asked, still looking rather sick at what had happened here.

Dani shook her head. "No. We've had quarrels, but never like this. He's never lost his temper with me like that before. Like I said, I lost mine, too."

"What happened?"

Dani shot a quick look at Mark, then lifted her chin defiantly. "I told him that he had to make a choice. His wife or me. I said the next time he showed up here, he'd better be holding divorce papers. That made him get all defensive and defiant and when he started to leave, I—I jumped in front of the door and called him a…a coward and a liar. And that made him so mad, he just—he just lost his temper. I think he wanted to stay to apologize but I told him to get out and he did. And that's when I called you, Rachel. I didn't know you were with him," she added with another look at Mark.

Mark wasn't sure what he'd done to get on her bad side. As far as he knew he'd been perfectly polite to her the one time they'd met previously. He remembered her scathing comment about Rachel dating doctors and lawyers while she was dating a married salesman, but that seemed like a rather shaky basis to take such a dislike to him.

"You should be glad I was with him," Rachel retorted. "If Mark hadn't been here to take care of you, I probably would have called an ambulance. At the very least, I'd have forced you into my car and driven you to the nearest emergency room. You have no idea how bad you looked when you opened that door."

"I should have washed my face," Dani muttered. "But I was so upset, I couldn't seem to think straight. I couldn't believe Kurt—"

Her voice trailed off, but it wasn't really necessary for her to finish the sentence.

Rachel shook her head. "Please tell me you aren't going to ever let him in here again."

The way Dani hesitated made both Rachel and Mark frown. "Dani?"

"I don't know if he'll even want to come back," Dani said with a glum shrug. "He was so angry when he left."

"And if he does come back?"

"I guess that depends on what he has to say."

"Damn it, Dani." Rachel pushed both hands through her hair in frustration.

Dani's eyes filled again. "You don't understand. I love him."

Making a sound of disgust, Rachel half turned away. "Get over it. He doesn't deserve it."

"That's easier said than done. I'm not like you. I can't just move on when a relationship—or even a marriage—ends."

Mark winced.

Rachel whirled back around. "Look, did you just call me so you could make digs at me? Or did you want me to help you?"

"I just…I needed you to be here for me. I didn't want a lecture."

"Okay, I'm here. What do you want me to do?"

Dani slumped and buried her face in her hands. "Never mind. Just leave me alone."

Softening, Rachel knelt beside her to stroke her hair. "Why don't you come home with me? You can spend the night with me and we'll talk."

"No. Thanks, but I'd rather stay here."

"Then I'll stay with you here. You can take me to Mark's for my car tomorrow."

"No. I just need some time by myself. I'll talk to you tomorrow, okay?"

Rachel looked worried. "I don't know if that's such a good idea."

Mark suspected that Rachel was afraid to leave her sister alone in case Kurt came back. And he had the same concern. "Why don't you let her stay, Dani? I'll clear out. I'm sure the two of you would like to be alone together to talk. Her car's fine at my place for tonight."

Rachel gave him a look of gratitude for the effort, though she knew he'd regret that their own time together would be cut short yet again.

But Dani shook her head once more, a new look of resolution on her bruised face. "I really need some time alone," she repeated. "I have to think for myself on this."

"What if he comes back?" Rachel finally asked bluntly.

"He won't come back tonight. And if he does, I'll tell him the same thing I'm telling you. I need to be alone to think. I won't let him in."

Rachel so obviously wanted to argue more, but Dani had made up her mind.

"Promise me you won't say anything about this to Mother," she insisted as she all but pushed them toward the door.

"She's going to see your face, Dani. Mother's not stupid."

"I'll avoid her until the bruise fades. Maybe I'll go to Macon to visit my friend Lynne for a few days. I haven't see her in a while. I'll take some time off from my job and the cantina. I've got vacation days."

Rachel bit her lip, then said, "You're running."

"Maybe. For a little while. I just don't want Mother to know about this. You know it's best, Ray-Ray. You know how she would overreact."

Sighing, Rachel said, "I won't tell her. Not now, anyway."

Though Rachel tried again to talk Dani into letting her stay, Dani remained insistent that they leave. Minutes later, Rachel and Mark were in his car.

She looked over her shoulder as he drove toward the parking lot exit. He braked before turning onto the street. "Do you want to go back?"

"No." She shook her head. "She doesn't want me to stay. I don't know why she called me in the first place."

He thought he understood. Dani had been shocked and upset by her boyfriend's attack. Her first impulse, as always, had been to call the sister who could always be counted on to drop everything and rush to her side. Having him show up with Rachel had been embarrassing for Dani, which had made her turn defensive and uncooperative.

Personally, he thought it was good for Dani to see that Rachel had a life outside the family. She couldn't continue to bail out her siblings every time their reckless choices got them into trouble. But this wasn't the time to say anything along those lines to Rachel, not while she was still shaken from seeing her sister with blood running down her face and tear-swollen eyes.

They didn't say much more during the drive to his house. Mark wanted to assure her that Dani would be all right, but he couldn't be certain of that himself just then. He wanted to believe that Dani had enough spunk to dump Kurt once and for all after this, but he'd known a couple of very bright, capable and otherwise strong women who had gotten tangled up in abusive situations they couldn't seem to end.

At least he'd been spared that as a kid, he thought with a tinge of bitterness. His mother, or the woman he'd thought of in that respect, had never dated. Except for him, she'd kept to herself almost reclusively. Had she been afraid that getting too close to anyone else would lead to the discovery of what she had done?

He found that he still couldn't think of her. Focusing on Rachel instead, he asked as he drove into his garage, "You'll come in, won't you?"

"I—"

"We'll order pizza," he said enticingly. "I'll let you decorate something."

She smiled at that, though it was a bit shaky. "You do know my weaknesses, don't you?"

"A few of them." And he hoped to learn the rest in time.

While Rachel went to wash up inside, he dialed his favorite pizza delivery restaurant and ordered a large with the toppings she'd said she liked. He had barely hung up when the phone rang in his hand. Seeing Ethan's number, he lifted the phone to his ear again. "Hello?"

"I told them today."

"All of them?"

"Yes. I asked Joel and Nic to come to Danston so they could all hear at once."

"How did they take it?"

"About like you'd expect. They were stunned. Angry at what had been stolen from them and from you. Sad about the lost years. And now they're all anxious to meet you."

Mark swallowed. "When?"

"It's your decision. You still want to do it there?"

Maybe it was cowardly of him, maybe even a bit selfish, since he was asking an entire family to travel for his convenience, but he still said, "Yes. That would be best for me, if it works for everyone else."

"You should have figured out by now that they would travel to the other side of the world to meet you, Mark."

Mark didn't know what to say to that.

"So, when do you want us? Everyone's prepared to come

whenever it's convenient for you. Of course, Mom and Dad wanted to get on a plane tonight, but I talked them into letting me make the arrangements with you first."

"Um, this weekend, maybe? That'll give everyone the rest of the week to make travel plans, and I can get the house ready for company. I, uh—everyone can stay here, of course. I've got enough bedrooms."

"That's a very generous invitation. You're sure?"

"Of course." It was an offer he hoped he wouldn't regret.

"I'll call and let you know the arrangements."

"Yeah, okay. So...bye, Ethan."

Rachel stood in the kitchen doorway when he disconnected the call. She had obviously heard enough to know what was going on. "They're coming this weekend?"

He cleared his throat. "Yes."

"Then I guess we have a lot of work to do, don't we?"

He appreciated her matter-of-fact tone. "Yeah. I guess we do."

Chapter Thirteen

His house was a whirlwind of activity when Mark got home from work Friday. It was well after five, but the whole crew was still there, cars and pickup trucks lined up in the driveway, people bustling through the hallways like drones in an anthill. Rachel played the part of queen, giving orders and rushing from room to room to make sure those orders were followed exactly to her specifications.

Unnoticed in the commotion, Mark stood back and watched for a few minutes, amused by her intense concentration. She was determined to have the house in shape for his weekend company and she was working overtime—and making sure everyone else did, too—to see that it happened.

She broke into a smile when she saw him. "Well?" she said. "What do you think?"

He looked around the guest room in which he'd found her. This was the smallest of the rooms, and they'd decorated it with a simple platform bed, a nightstand with a bookshelf built into the bottom, a small chest of drawers topped by an oval mirror and a parson's chair with a rattan magazine basket full of magazines beside it. The woods were medium-stained, the linens tone-on-tone cream striped. Earthy colored throw pillows were arranged on the bed. Botanical prints hung on the walls, adding a bit more color.

A brass reading lamp and a vase of fresh flowers sat on the nightstand and several hardcover books were lined up on the shelf. Rachel had truly thought of everything to make his guests comfortable, he thought, knowing that the bathrooms were stocked with coordinated towels and assortments of soaps and lotions.

"It looks great," he said. "Really nice."

She looked pleased. "I've got just a couple of things left to do in here, then I'm going to do a walk-through of the entire house to make sure I haven't forgotten anything for tomorrow."

"I'll take that walk with you. Just let me step into my room and change first."

She nodded and turned back to the window, where two young men were hanging a brass curtain rod on which she would drape the cream-colored window scarf she'd selected for this room.

Tugging at his tie, he walked down the hallway that wrapped around the top of the staircase and led into his bedroom. The door was open and he heard someone moving around in the lounge, which was still only partially furnished since the couch and leather chair hadn't yet arrived. He took the two steps down into the dressing room and walked into the lounge to find Rachel's younger brother there, sprawled on the one chair that had already been delivered and watching the TV over the fireplace.

Clay stumbled to his feet when Mark came in, turning off the TV and tossing the remote onto the table where he'd found it. "Oh. Hey. I was just…uh…"

"Hiding out?" Mark finished smoothly.

"Nah. Taking a break. I brought in that floor lamp like Rachel told me to and I just sat down for a minute."

Mark nodded. "So, how's it been going? Do you like your new job?"

The boy shrugged. "It's kind of boring. But it's okay, I guess."

"You're about to take some more college classes?"

"I'll take a couple in the fall. Just required stuff."

"What's your major?"

Clay shrugged again. "Haven't declared one yet."

"What do you want to do? Not work on a remodeling crew, apparently."

"I don't know. Pretty much all jobs are boring, really."

"That's mostly a matter of attitude. If you approach it the right way, any job can be interesting. The one you're doing now, for example. Rachel needs you to give it your best. She counts on her crew to keep up her professional reputation. I know you want to help her with that. She certainly deserves to be successful at this career she loves so much."

"Yeah. I guess." Clay glanced at the door as if wondering if he could make a quick escape.

"Gotta be tough on you," Mark commented, shrugging out of his jacket and tossing it over the back of the single chair. "Being the only man responsible for so many women, I mean. Your grandmother, your mother, your two sisters. Must be a load on your mind."

"Uh—I'm not exactly responsible for them. They pretty much take care of themselves."

"Oh, yeah, they all seem independent enough. But every family needs an anchor, you know? Someone they can always count on when they're in trouble. Someone who'll step in and take charge when necessary."

The boy pushed his hands into the pockets of his faded jeans. "Sounds like you're describing Rachel."

"Think she ever gets tired of running to the rescue? She's

probably looked forward to the day when her little brother would grow up enough to help her with the responsibilities."

Scowling, Clay looked at him suspiciously. "Are you making cracks about me?"

"Hey, I'm just commenting. I grew up with a single mother, myself, and she had to work two jobs sometimes just to keep a roof over our heads. I had to pretty much take care of her from the time I was old enough to help out—I must have been eleven, maybe twelve when I got my first part-time job. I was on my own by the time I was just a couple years older than you. She died in a car accident. You've had it pretty good so far. Your mom and your sisters taking care of you, letting you stay a kid. But I'd think you'd be getting impatient now to have them see you as a man, not a little boy."

Clay drew himself up to his full height, his eyes narrowing. "I'm not a kid."

"I know that. Which is why I'm talking to you man-to-man. They're the ones who still treat you like a boy who needs constant supervision. It's hard to break a lifetime of habits, I guess. For all of you."

"I do get tired of them acting like I'm a kid," Clay admitted reluctantly. "I don't know how to convince them I'm not one, anymore."

Mark's first impulse was to tell him to stop acting like one. But he tried to phrase the advice more tactfully. "Guess you just have to prove it. You know, start giving them less reason to worry about you. Make some decisions about your future and start working toward them. Maybe see if you can do something to help them for a change, instead of the other way around all the time."

"Like any of them need help."

Mark lifted an eyebrow. "Have you paid much attention to Dani lately?"

"Dani? No, not really. Why?"

"So I guess she left town before you saw the black eye." He

knew he was treading a fine line there, and that both Dani and
Rachel would probably be annoyed with him for even hinting to
Clay what had happened.

Clay stiffened. "Dani had a black eye?"

"Yeah. A bad one. I treated it the best I could."

Shock turned to temper in the boy's brown eyes. "Who did
it? That jerk she's been dating? The one Mom doesn't like?"

Mark nodded.

His fists clenching, Clay growled, "I'll pound him."

"That isn't what your family needs right now. I think Dani can
take care of herself once she sees the guy for who he is—and I
believe she's coming around to that. You might want to stay
apprised of the situation as much as you can without butting in,
but there's no need to upset your mother or grandmother about
it. Dani doesn't want them to know."

"She didn't want me to know, either, did she?"

Mark shrugged, looking steadily at the young man. "Maybe
she was still trying to protect you, too. That baby brother thing.
Or maybe she just didn't think you would care."

"Then she was wrong."

"Rachel's got a lot to worry about right now. Her new
business. Dani. Her mother and grandmother. You."

"She doesn't need to be worrying about me," Clay muttered.

"Doesn't she?"

Flushing, Clay shook his shaggy head. "No."

Mark smiled. "I didn't think so. I had a feeling the first time
I met you that you're a man who's been getting frustrated with
his situation and just didn't know how to change it. Hurts not
having a dad around to talk to, doesn't it? I grew up without one,
too, you know."

His jaw clenching as a sign of his lingering grief over his
father's untimely death, Clay nodded.

"Look, Clay, I sure don't have all the answers. Hell, my life's
so complicated right now I've lost track of most of the questions.

But if you ever need another man to just talk things over with, you know where to find me, okay? Maybe we can go fishing sometime. You like to fish?"

"I used to fish with my dad when I was a kid. I haven't been since he died."

"I haven't had a chance lately, myself. It would be nice having someone to go with."

"Yeah, okay. Maybe," Clay added, not wanting to look too eager.

"That's great. I'll call you, and we'll set up a time."

"Okay. Sure. If I'm free."

"Of course."

"There you guys are. I was wondering what happened to you," Rachel said, entering the lounge with a curious expression. "Everyone's packing up to leave, Clay."

Mark answered the question he saw in her eyes. "Clay and I were just talking. You know. Man stuff."

Rachel laughed and pushed a hand through her hair. Mark noticed that Clay was giving his sister a hard look, and he wondered if the young man was suddenly noticing just how tired she looked after her long, very busy week.

"Man stuff, huh?" she asked. "Like spitting and scratching?"

"And belching," Mark added with a grin. "Don't forget that."

"Of course."

Clay moved toward the doorway, pausing in front of his sister. "I'm going down to help the guys clean up. I've got plans with my friends tonight, but you don't have to worry. I won't do anything stupid."

Though she looked a little surprised, Rachel nodded. "That's good to hear. Do you need any money or anything?"

He stood taller again. "No. I have my own money. But thanks, anyway, sis. Call me if you need anything, okay?"

"Um…sure. Thanks, Clay."

She turned to Mark with her hands on her hips. "What was that all about?"

"I think he's trying to let you know that you should all stop treating him like a dependent child."

"Excuse me?"

"He's nineteen, Rachel. You keep saying he needs to grow up, but you aren't letting him. Asking him if he needs money? In front of me? How can he feel like a man when you treat him like a little boy?"

A wave of color flooded her cheeks. "I didn't think—"

"I know. But maybe you should start thinking when it comes to Clay. You can't keep babying him. Bailing him out. Making excuses for him. You have to let him step up. Grow up. Learn from his own mistakes and successes."

Defenses kicking in, she lifted her chin. "You've certainly had a lot of advice about my family lately."

"You can give it but can't take it?"

She drew a deep breath. "Maybe we'd better walk through your house now."

Before they got into a quarrel, she might as well have added. And maybe he was primed for an argument with her, for some reason, because it took him a moment to nod and say, "Fine. I can change clothes later."

Everyone else had cleared out quickly, leaving them alone in his house. They passed the small bedroom in which he'd found her earlier and looked into the other two guest rooms. Identically sized, they both opened into a little hallway that led into the guest bath.

The first was furnished with an iron bed finished in antique brass. A hand-pieced Lone Star quilt in reds, blues and creams served as a bedspread over a simple cream bed skirt. The shams matched the quilt and a couple of throw pillows were covered in solid colors pulled from the quilt's design. A dusky-blue chenille throw draped artfully over the iron footboard. In lieu of a nightstand, Rachel had set a large round woven tray on a rattan luggage rack, topping it with a small lamp and a thriving English ivy in a glazed ceramic pot.

The chest was an antique, as was the mirror above it; both were pieces they had discovered on one of their shopping outings. An old rocker sat in one corner of the room, and a small, repro-duction antique writing desk in another. The desk held a couple of carelessly stacked books and a fat scented candle. Folksy art hung on the walls and a few more antique store finds had been cleverly placed here and there.

They'd found a mahogany sleigh bed for the final bedroom, dressing it in another hand-pieced quilt, this one in a multicol-ored Log Cabin pattern. Again, Rachel had used colors from the quilt for her selection of the pillows and throw. The mahogany side tables were oval-shaped, with three glass shelves on which she'd arranged candles, books and tissues. The lamp bases were a pale blue ceramic.

A dresser with an attached mirror sat on one wall, a small vanity with a stool on another. An armchair and footstool sat by the windows, the chair made of mahogany with rattan inserts and cushioned in a cranberry-red fabric. It was another warm, wel-coming room, and Rachel's special touches had made it that way, he thought, glancing at the fresh flowers and the crystal candy dish filled with peppermints that was on the dresser.

"Everything looks great," he said, turning to look at her. "You've really knocked yourself out the last couple of days. Thank you."

She nodded as some of the tension left her body. "You're welcome. I know you wanted it to look nice when your family arrives."

"I saw the office when I came in. It looks great. Exactly what I wanted."

"I'm glad. You'll have to arrange your books and files the way you want them, of course, but I placed everything where I thought it would work for now. Marty hooked up all your new office equipment. He's good at that sort of thing."

He'd noticed that when he'd looked into the doorway of the

masculine-style office with its espresso-finished office furniture, built-in bookcases, brass lamps and decorative globes and a big, framed collector's map over the fireplace. Even in the office, she'd thought of his comfort, talking him into tucking a window seat/daybed beneath the windows, made inviting with throw pillows and made practical with rattan baskets lined up in three open storage compartments beneath.

With the exception of a few pieces still on order, his house was basically furnished and decorated. It had been done quickly, efficiently and expensively, of course, by the time he'd paid for express delivery on some of the items. But it was worth it, he thought, looking around the house that he had worked so hard and saved so long to buy. The home he had wanted all his life.

He had fantasized vaguely about starting a new family in this house. Funny how life had a way of twisting reality, he thought with a smile.

Rachel was looking at him oddly now, as if wondering what he was thinking. "Are you ready to go downstairs for a check down there?" she asked.

"Almost." He moved toward her, raising his hands to cup her face between them. "It just occurred to me that I haven't even kissed you today, after all you've done for me."

She smiled up at him. "I think that can be remedied."

Bending his head, he caught her lower lip gently between his teeth, wanting to taste her smile. And because that brief nip wasn't nearly enough to satisfy him, he went back for more, greedily taking her mouth.

She crowded against him, her hands running across his chest, creeping over his shoulders, her legs tangling with his. Mark settled his hands on her hips, holding her even more closely against him, his mouth moving feverishly against hers.

They stumbled together into his bedroom. Clothes falling heedlessly to the floor, they tumbled onto the bed. Whether fueled by the hours that had passed since they'd last been together or by the tempers that had flared so briefly earlier, the heat between them was intense, consuming. They threw themselves willingly, recklessly into the flames.

"We should probably get out of this bed eventually," Rachel murmured, nestling her head into Mark's shoulder.

He smoothed the covers over them. "Why?"

"Food? Checking the rest of the house in preparation for your company? Just because we should?"

He chuckled. "We'll get to all of that. Eventually."

Scooting back from him just a little, she propped her head up on one arm and gazed down at him. He looked so good lying there against the sheets she had selected for him, she decided, running a fingertip across his sleek, broad chest. "You're a lovely man, Mark Thomas."

He frowned, his hand stilling where he'd been stroking her bare arm. "Lovely?"

She laughed. "I didn't mean to impugn your masculinity. I just think you're beautiful."

"Thank you. I think. And it's quite mutual, by the way."

She leaned down to kiss him quickly, then pulled back again. "So," she said, her hand spread on his chest, "are you getting excited about tomorrow?"

Something in his eyes changed. Darkened.

"Excited?" He shrugged against the pillows. "I'm not sure that's the word I would use."

"What word *would* you use?"

"Oh, I don't know. Dread, maybe. It's going to be pretty awkward."

"At first. I'm sure it will get better as you start to think of them as your family."

"You act like that's going to be so easy."

"No." She shook her head firmly. "I never said it would be

easy. I just said it will happen, eventually. At least, I hope so, for everyone's sake."

He rubbed her arm again, his gaze following the slow path of his hand. "Do you have plans for tomorrow?"

She felt the tingles trailing behind his fingertips, all the way up to her shoulder. "Not specifically."

"Will you be here to meet them with me?"

She tried to meet his eyes, but he was still looking at her arm. "Why do you want me here?"

"I always want you here," he answered simply.

They both knew there was more to it than that. "I'm not sure how I feel about being used as a buffer between you and your family."

That brought his gaze to hers. "I'm not using you for anything," he said with a bit too much emphasis. "It was just an invitation. It would be nice to have you here, but I can handle it on my own, if I need to."

She was a bit taken aback by his vehemence. "Of course you can. I didn't mean—"

He sighed, his fingers tightening briefly on her forearm. "I'm sorry. I guess I am a bit nervous about the whole thing."

"I'm sure you are. And I would love to meet your family, if you don't think that would make things even more awkward."

"Why would it?"

"Well, I mean—I'm your decorator," she said, grimacing as she heard how lame it sounded.

He laughed softly, his breath caressing her face. "You're a lot more than that. I think anyone who sees us together will figure that out pretty quickly."

Stroking her lips against his, she murmured, "Let's just be glad no one can see us now."

But as she sank into another long, lazy kiss with him, she couldn't help wondering exactly how he saw her in his life, now that the decorating job was at an end.

A while later, Mark released a long, regretful breath. "I'm

getting hungry. Guess we should think about dinner before long. Want to go out?"

"Sure." Tucked into his side again, she looked up at the ceiling. "It will be nice to see Ethan again. You said Aislinn can't come?"

"No. She had too many obligations with her cake decorating business this weekend."

"That's a shame. I'd like to see her again."

"Me, too, I guess. Even if she is a little spooky."

She laughed. "A little."

He tangled his fingers in her hair. "So, what do you want to eat tonight? Italian? Greek? Chinese? Ethiopian?"

"It all sounds good. Though I have to admit Greek food isn't my favorite."

"Really? My mom loved it. Even though she wasn't Greek, she made the best moussaka I ever—" He stopped abruptly.

Rachel lifted her head. Stricken by the expression on his face, she placed a hand on his cheek. "It's okay to remember her, you know," she said quietly. "She was the only mother you knew."

He planted a kiss in her palm, then rolled her gently aside as he scooted toward the edge of the bed. "I'm going to take a shower before dinner. I'm in the mood for Chinese tonight, I think. I discovered a new place recently that makes the best kung pao chicken. It's casual, so you don't have to worry about wearing the same clothes you had on earlier."

Struggling up to her elbows, Rachel held the sheet to her chest and frowned as he grabbed his clothes off the floor and headed for the bathroom. "Mark, wait. Don't you want to talk about this?"

"No." He paused in the doorway, looking back at her. "I don't."

With that, he closed the door firmly between them. Her chest tightening painfully, Rachel felt as if he'd just shut her out in more ways than one.

Letting the hot water run over his head and down onto his face, Mark braced himself against the shower wall with one hand, his shoulders bowed into the spray. Even as the water sluiced away the sweat and dust of the day, he wished it could wash away the memories in his head. Not to mention the pain in his heart.

And even though the woman of his dreams was in his bed and his newfound family would descend on him in less than twenty-four hours, he felt very much alone at that moment.

Mark was pacing Saturday morning, back and forth across the gathering room, prowling like a caged cat. Having made last-minute adjustments to nearly every item in the house, Rachel had nothing left to do to help prepare for his guests, who were due to arrive at any time. She wished she knew how to help him prepare himself.

"Mark," she said, stepping in front of him when he turned to make another lap around the room. "You must have walked ten miles in the past half hour. Wouldn't you like to sit down for a few minutes?"

He gave her a rather sheepish smile. "I guess I'm a little keyed up."

Wrapping her arms around his neck, she kissed his chin. "I noticed."

"Did I thank you for being here for me today?" he asked, sliding his arms around her waist.

"You did. More than once."

"Okay. Thank you again." He pressed his mouth to hers. She couldn't help noticing that his lips were drier than usual, due, no doubt, to nerves, but she certainly wasn't complaining.

The doorbell rang, and Mark went tense against her. She watched his throat work with a hard swallow when he stepped back. "I guess that's them."

She nodded. "I'm sure it is. Why don't I let them in? It would be easier for you to meet them in here than in the foyer."

He jumped quickly on the momentary reprieve. "Yeah. All right. Thanks."

She patted his shoulder on the way past. "It will be okay, Mark."

"Yeah." He sounded grim as he agreed. "Of course it will."

She smoothed a hand down the front of her sleeveless top and full cotton skirt as she walked into the stone-floored foyer. She had debated what to wear on this hot, late-summer afternoon, and had finally decided that bright and casual would best set the tone for this meeting. Not that there was anything casual about it, she thought, opening the door.

Ethan had been the one to ring the bell. He stood in front of the group, looking only mildly surprised that she had been the one to answer. "Hello, Rachel. It's good to see you again."

"You, too, Ethan. I'm sorry Aislinn couldn't be here."

"She said to tell you hello. She knew I would see you, of course."

She smiled. "Of course. Please, everyone, come in. I'm Mark's friend, Rachel Madison. Mark is waiting for us in the den."

The two couples with Ethan both walked in hand in hand. She studied them as they entered. Joel looked enough like Ethan and Mark that there was no doubt he was their brother, though his eyes were more hazel than the vivid green of his brothers'. His wife, Nic, the police officer, was girl-next-door cute with a fresh face and dark blond hair worn in a casually shaggy style.

The boys had inherited their looks from their father, Dr. Lou Brannon, an older, slightly heavier version of them with thinning hair and metal-framed glasses. His wife, Elaine, was a petite ash blonde who looked understandably pale and anxious. She paused in front of Rachel. "Is he…how does he feel about meeting us?"

Rachel smiled reassuringly at the woman, touched by the suffering she saw in the lightly lined face. "He's nervous, of course. But he's ready to meet you all."

"He's okay?"

Feeling her heart melt, Rachel touched the older woman's shoulder. "He's fine."

It wasn't exactly the truth, she thought as she stepped back to lead the family toward the gathering room. Mark was suffering, too.

Maybe he would tell his new family about his feelings. He certainly hadn't shown any desire to do so with her. He had shared his bed with her, but she was painfully aware that he had shared little else.

Chapter Fourteen

Mark had steeled himself for the possibility, but it still shook him when the petite, fragile-looking woman he assumed was his mother burst into tears at the first sight of him.

"I'm so sorry," she said brokenly, gazing up at him with her hands clenched and pressed against her chest. "I told myself I wouldn't do this."

"It's all right. I understand," Mark assured her.

Draping his left arm around his mother's shoulders, Ethan reached out with his right hand to Mark. "We all knew this was going to be tough," he murmured.

Aware that he was being closely scrutinized by everyone in the room, Mark shook the offered hand. "It's good to see you, Ethan."

"I guess it's up to me to make the introductions." Ethan smiled faintly down at his mother. "And remember, everyone, he prefers to answer to Mark now. It's the only name he remembers using. This, of course, is Mom. Elaine Brannon."

Mark wasn't quite sure whether to offer a hand or a cheek or what to his mother, but Elaine solved that problem by reaching out to take both his hands in her smaller, icier ones. "You're so handsome," she said, still memorizing his face. "I can tell by looking at you that you've grown into a fine young man. We have so much lost time to catch up on."

He cleared his throat, trying to keep his emotions banked so that he could speak coherently. "We've got all weekend to talk."

Her smile was wobbly. "It won't be enough."

Ethan moved her very gently aside. "Let Dad get a chance to meet him," he said.

Dr. Lou Brannon took his place in front of Mark and offered a hand somewhat awkwardly. "Hello, Mark."

Unfortunately, Mark had no idea what to call this man he was laying eyes on for the first time in his memory. He settled for, "Sir."

Clutching Mark's hand tightly, Lou said, "I want you to know that I looked for you, son. Every single day for more than a year. Had I known, had there been any question in my mind that you were still alive, I would have done everything in my power to find you."

Mark nodded. "I know. From what Ethan told me, there was no reason for you to think I was still alive."

Squeezing his father's shoulder, Ethan nodded toward the final members of the family. "This is Joel, and his wife, Nic."

Joel shook Mark's hand warmly, clapping his arm at the same time. "You and I will have to compare medical school and residency horror stories sometime this weekend. Yours should still be fresh in your mind."

"Still fresh enough to give me nightmares," Mark replied, grateful for the light tone.

He turned to Nic, his hand still extended. She gave it a firm shake. "Welcome to the family. I'm new, too, but I already feel like one of the clan. Especially since my best friend, Aislinn, is joining up in a couple of months."

He laughed. "Joining up? You make it sound like the military."

"Cop talk," she confessed with a shrug.

Rachel stepped forward then. "Why don't you all sit down so you can talk. I bet you're thirsty after traveling all morning. There's iced tea in the fridge, or a fresh pot of coffee. What can I get everyone?"

She had offered earlier to help Mark with this meeting by serving as hostess and leaving him to concentrate on conversation. He'd agreed appreciatively, knowing he would be too preoccupied to think of the little courtesies of being a host. He gave her a smile. "Did everyone meet Rachel?"

"I introduced them," Ethan explained, sitting on one end of the sectional sofa.

"Let me help you with the refreshments," Nic offered, moving to the doorway with Rachel. "You guys go ahead and talk. We'll be right back."

The rest of the family took their seats on the long sofa, Elaine still dabbing at her eyes with a tissue as she sat close to her husband. Mark took a chair facing them, feeling a bit as if he were on display there. Everyone kept looking at him. He supposed he couldn't blame them, but it made him self-conscious.

Ethan made the first attempt to break the tension, as uncomfortable with the heavy emotions as Mark. "Your house looks great, Mark. You've gotten a lot done since I was here last."

"Thanks to Rachel," he agreed. "She's had her whole crew working overtime this past week. Rachel's a professional decorator," he added for the rest of the family's benefit. "She did the whole house. I just bought it recently and I thought I needed help choosing the furniture and colors and stuff."

"She's very good," Elaine said, looking around the room for the first time. "It looks very warm and homey."

"That's what we were going for. I didn't want much formality."

"Ethan told us you've lived in Georgia ever since you were… taken from us," she murmured, her gaze turning back to him now. "We moved to Alabama more than twenty-five years ago, and we had no idea you were living only one state away all that time."

He spread his hands. "There was no way you could have known."

"Were you…were you happy, Ky—um, Mark?" she asked, with a slight stammer over the name.

This was the hard part for him. He could hardly bear to think of his childhood now that he knew the truth, but he knew they would want—need—to know the details. "I was happy enough," he assured her. "I was on my own a lot. She worked several minimum-wage jobs to support us. She said we didn't have any other family, so it was always just the two of us."

Elaine was crying again, silently, but heart-wrenchingly. "Was she good to you?"

"Yes," he answered a bit gruffly. "She never let me lack for anything I really needed."

"Except your family," Joel muttered, looking angry now.

Mark couldn't respond to that.

"You never knew? Never suspected that she wasn't really your mother?" Lou asked, his expression bewildered.

"No. I never even thought to wonder. I mean, I thought it was odd that she had no family at all, that she would never talk about my father, who she said died before I was born, and that she didn't have any real friends of her own, even though she wanted me to be popular in school. I just always believed she was extremely shy and embarrassed about her lack of education and the blue-collar jobs she worked."

Lou ran a hand over his lined face. "I can't imagine why she did what she did. We were very fond of her. She could have worked for us for several more years and stayed friends with the family afterward. She didn't have to take you away to remain a part of your life."

Mark looked down at his hands, realized they were clenched, and made a deliberate effort to relax them. "I don't know why she did it. She's been dead for years. She didn't leave a convenient note or diary entry, the way Aislinn's mother did. No deathbed confessions. She took her secrets to the grave with her."

"Obviously she wanted Mark to herself," Ethan said with a slight shrug. "She didn't want him to know her as his nanny, but as his mother. It was a completely selfish act."

"She was obviously a very disturbed woman," Joel chimed in. "Did she show any signs of mental illness during the years you were with her, Mark?"

"She suffered from some depression," he admitted. "I can understand that more now, I suppose. But on the whole, she seemed like the average mother, if somewhat more introverted. She went to all my school stuff, met with the teachers, joined the PTA—though she was never a leader in anything, more just a silent participant."

Because it was becoming too painful, he asked rather abruptly, "Would you mind if we don't talk about her anymore right now? I mean, I just don't have that many answers for you when it comes to her."

A brief silence followed his request, mercifully broken when Rachel and Nic reentered the room, laughing like old friends and carrying trays of refreshments. Iced tea for everyone but Lou, who'd asked for a cup of coffee, and little pecan cookies Rachel had brought with her that morning.

"You two seem to be getting along well," Joel remarked, standing to help them set the trays on the chest that served as a coffee table.

"Did you know Rachel decorated this entire house? She and Mark chose everything together and she arranged it all. You should see the kitchen and dining room. They're amazing."

"Mark was just telling us that you helped him decorate," Elaine said with a smile as Rachel handed her a glass. "But you're more than a decorator to him. I can tell."

Rachel glanced at Mark, who had stood when she entered. He slipped an arm around her waist. "Yes, she's much more than a decorator to me."

Glancing up at him through her lashes, Rachel gave him a look he couldn't quite interpret.

"Tell us about your new partnership, Mark," Nic said to start the conversation rolling again. "Ethan told us you're in a family practice clinic?"

He nodded and began to tell them everything he could about his life at that time. The others listened and commented appropriately, though he was aware that neither of his parents took their eyes off his face for a moment. Almost as if he might disappear again if they did, he thought with an odd pang in his chest.

Mark showed everyone upstairs a short while later, helping them carry their bags to the rooms he and Rachel had selected for them. From the bottom of the stairs, Rachel could hear them talking, exclaiming about the decorating of the guest rooms, still asking Mark questions and telling him about themselves.

The visit was going fairly well, she thought, resisting an impulse to cross her fingers. Though emotions had run high since the family had arrived, they'd managed to keep them under control. Mark was being courteous, if a bit more reserved than usual, while the others were making a visible effort not to over-whelm him with their feelings about being reunited with him. That, of course, seemed most difficult for his mother, but she, too, had kept herself mostly under control.

It had to hurt Elaine to know that he was still having a hard time thinking of her as his mother, rather than a nice woman he had only just met.

Rachel and Mark had planned a nice lunch for the family. She had offered to help serve a casual, cold meal that they had pre-assembled and was now waiting in the refrigerator. He was taking them all out for dinner that evening at his favorite Italian restaurant, figuring they would be ready for a diversion by that time.

He was glad Rachel was there. Every time he looked at her she could tell that he was grateful for her presence. When he had put his arm around her, it had been as if he were clinging to a familiar lifeline in uncharted seas. And while her eager-to-be-ofservice nature found gratification in knowing she could help him this way, she still wondered exactly what she meant to him other than a temporary ally.

After his family left, they were going to have to talk, she thought, glancing toward the stairs again. Especially now that their professional connection was coming to an end.

Her cell phone vibrated at her waist and she sighed, thinking that at least she'd had an uninterrupted morning. She hoped this would be something easily handled by phone, since she was planning to serve lunch soon.

The name on the ID screen made her frown. She walked into Mark's office to take the call. "Kaylee? Hi, what's up?"

Deep, gulping sobs were her only answer.

"Kaylee?" Though Rachel was used to the other woman's dramatics, she couldn't help but be worried by the vehemence of the crying this time. "What's wrong? Are you okay?"

"It's—it's Robbie," Kaylee gasped out. "Oh, Rachel."

"Robbie? Oh, God, has something happened to Robbie?"

"He—he left me," Kaylee wailed. "He said he isn't coming back."

Sagging a little in relief that the news wasn't more tragic, Rachel spoke soothingly, "Now, Kaylee, you and Robbie have had fights before. He's just trying to shake you up. You know he'll come back."

"No. It's different this time. You didn't see his face. He looked so cold and hard. I've never seen him like that. He said he's sick of the restaurant and sick of me and that he just wants to start over somewhere on his own. I don't even know where he is. He won't answer his cell phone."

Rubbing her suddenly aching forehead, Rachel said, "What is it that you want me to do, exactly, Kaylee?"

"You've got to talk to him before he does something crazy! What if he kills himself or something? Oh, Rachel—" And she burst into a fresh round of noisy weeping, making Rachel wince and hold the phone a little farther away from her ear. "Please, you've got to come. Please?"

"I really can't come now. I have other obligations."

"I don't know what to do. Oh, God, I'll kill myself if something happens to him."

"Nothing's going to happen to him, Kaylee. He's just mad."

"I really need you to come, Rachel. He'll listen to you. I think he wishes he never left you to marry me."

"That's not true. Robbie was never as happy with me as he has been with you. He's upset right now, but he'll cool down."

"You just don't care if anything happens to him. You hate me, don't you? You think it's my fault that Robbie's so miserable. You think I'm a terrible wife to him."

Rachel finally broke into the increasingly frenzied diatribe with a frustrated, "All right! Just stop. You're getting hysterical."

"You'll come?" Kaylee asked, hiccupping.

"I'll be there in a couple of hours."

Kaylee started crying again. "That could be too late."

Sighing heavily, Rachel squeezed the skin between her eyes. Mark was going to be annoyed with her, but she supposed she had no choice. "Okay. I'm on my way. Just don't do anything stupid before I get there, okay?"

"Thank you. Oh, thank you, Rachel. Please hurry."

Rachel closed her phone and then pounded it lightly against her forehead, silently calling herself a fool and a sucker. And then she turned toward the doorway…only to find Mark standing there, scowling at her. "You're leaving?"

"I'm sorry. I have to go."

He stepped into the room and closed the door deliberately behind him. "Who was it? Dani? Is she okay?"

"It wasn't Dani. Dani's still with her friend in Macon, and she's doing fine."

"Clay? Your mother?"

"No. It was Kaylee."

"Kaylee." He crossed his arms over his chest and studied her with a dispassion that made her stomach clench. "Your ex-husband's wife."

It wasn't a question, but she nodded, anyway. "She and Robbie had a big fight, and she's hysterical. She's afraid he's going to do something rash."

"So she called you."

"She doesn't really have anyone else to call. None of her family lives in this area and she doesn't have many close friends outside of the restaurant."

"Isn't it strange how you're always the only person for anyone to call when they're in trouble? What, exactly, would happen if—oh, I don't know—your cell phone battery died or something? Would the whole world just go to hell in a handbasket?"

Rachel bit her lip. Mark was more than annoyed. He was furious. She could see it in his eyes, and even though she had never really seen him in a temper before, she had no trouble identifying the emotion. "I'm sorry. I didn't know what else to tell her."

"Did you ever consider telling her no? Or that you can't drop everything and run anytime someone has a problem they want you to solve for them?"

"I know you're upset because you're having a stressful day," she said, trying to be patient. "And I know you needed me to be here this morning, but I'm sure everything will be fine for lunch. I'll try to—"

"Let's get something straight." He stepped in front of her and looked her directly in the eyes. "I did not *need* you here this morning. I am perfectly capable of handling my family on my own."

Stung, she asked, "Then why did you ask me?"

"Because I wanted you here. And if you don't know the difference, then maybe you don't know me at all."

"How am I supposed to know you?" she retorted, planting her fists on her hips. "You won't talk to me about anything of importance to you. You won't discuss your past, or your feelings about what happened to you, or about the woman you thought was your mother. You've completely closed me out. So what am I to think, that you've been using me just like you accuse everyone else of doing? How do I know I haven't been just a convenient distraction to keep you from having to face your feelings about your family?"

"Maybe I didn't want to talk about those things because I didn't want to be just another one of your bleeding heart projects," he snapped. "Maybe I wanted to be the one person in your life who handled his own problems. But maybe that wasn't what you wanted. Maybe you're only interested in people you have to rescue. Maybe that gives you some sort of superiority rush."

"That," she said from between clenched teeth, "was unfair."

"Sorry," he said, though he didn't look it. "It's the best analysis I can make on the spur of the moment."

Holding her shoulders stiff, she moved toward the door. "Please tell your family I'm sorry I had to leave so abruptly. And that it was very nice meeting them all."

"Be sure to send me your final bills. I'll mail you a check."

"Fine."

"Fine."

She paused at the open doorway, her anger still too high to let her feel the pain she knew would come later. "You might ask yourself one thing after I go, Mark. Who were you really protecting by refusing to discuss your problems with me? Me—or yourself?"

She left the office door open behind her as she crossed the foyer toward the front door. She passed Ethan at the bottom of the stairs.

"Everything okay?" he asked, searching her expression.

"I've had a bit of an emergency come up, and I have to leave," she said, keeping her voice even with an effort. "It was nice to see you again, Ethan."

"Yeah, uh, you, too."

She was out the door and running for her car almost before he completed the sentence.

Rachel didn't want to go home to her empty apartment that evening, so she drove to her mother's house, instead. "This is a nice surprise," her mother said when she opened the door. "Come in. Have you had dinner?"

"Thanks, but I'm not hungry. I'd take a cup of tea, though."

"That sounds nice. I'll join you in a cup. Come into the kitchen and I'll boil some water."

Trailing her mother through the country kitsch that surrounded them, Rachel decided she had made the right decision to come here tonight. She had needed this, she thought sadly. "Where's Clay?"

"Oh, he's out on a date. A very nice young woman. He brought her by the house this afternoon so he could pick up a CD he was letting her borrow. She's a college sophomore. A prelaw major who's working in a law firm this summer. They met at a party last weekend. She seems very focused and levelheaded. Exactly what Clay needs. I know they've only started dating, but Clay seemed quite taken with her."

"I hope it works out for him, then." Taking a seat at the table, she watched her mother fill a cherry-red teakettle with water and place it on the stove. "How's Grandma? Have you talked to her today?"

"Oh, yes. She's fine. Tonight's her bingo night at the senior citizens' center."

With a little smile, Rachel said, "She does love her bingo."

Pulling two cat-decorated mugs off a mug tree, her mother set them on the counter and opened a cabinet to pull out a box of herbal teas. "Berry, mango or cinnamon apple?"

"Apple, please. Have you heard from Dani today?"

Her mother nodded somberly. "She called this afternoon.

She's going to stay with her friend a few more days. I think she's avoiding Kurt."

"Oh?" Rachel kept her expression unrevealing. "Why do you think that?"

"She told me she broke up with him and that he wasn't happy about it. I asked if she was sure it was over, and she told me absolutely, she won't be seeing him again. I told her how sorry I was that it didn't work out, but I really wanted to cheer," she admitted sheepishly. "I'm just so glad that's over. I know Dani can meet a nice man if she'd just be patient and hold out for someone who deserves her."

"Of course she will."

"You look tired, sweetie." Setting the steaming mugs on the table, her mother took a chair close to Rachel's. "You've been working too hard."

Rachel forced a smile. "I've just had a trying day." She told her about the frantic call from Kaylee, adding, "Robbie finally answered his phone and agreed to meet us in the restaurant office to talk. I think I convinced him that he and Kaylee really need a vacation. He's going to put up a sign saying that the restaurant will be closed the first week of September so they can take some time away to recharge. When he gets back, they're going to take my advice and hire a business consultant to look over their books and their work schedules. I'm sure they can stay afloat if they just make a few changes. Robbie has a loyal clientele."

Her mother shook her head in disapproval. "They shouldn't have put you in the middle that way. You don't have to keep running to your ex-husband's rescue, Rachel. He's never going to learn to handle his own problems if you don't stop taking care of things for him."

"Mmm. I think you're right. Of course, I could say the same thing about you and Clay—" she murmured.

Grimacing in acknowledgment of the direct hit, her mother nodded. "You're right," she startled Rachel by admitting. "It's time for Clay to grow up. Surprisingly enough, he's the one who told me it's time for me to stop treating him like a boy and let him take care of himself for a change. He said he's going to move into a dorm in the fall and take a full schedule of classes. He thinks it will be easier for him to learn to take responsibility if he isn't still living at home."

"How do you feel about that?"

Sighing, her mother answered, "Conflicted. On the one hand, I know he's right. On the other, well, I hate to admit that he's grown. That he doesn't need me anymore."

"Of course he needs you, Mother. He'll always need you, just as the rest of us do."

"I know. But it was my job to make sure you could all take care of yourselves. I did pretty well with you, but Dani and Clay have taken a bit longer to catch on—maybe because it took me longer to let them."

"Maybe." Rachel took a sip of her tea, thinking that she and her mother both needed to learn to curb their natural instincts to take care of everyone around them. Not because of anything Mark had said, of course, she added with a scowl.

"How's Mark?" her mother asked, as if hearing the thought. "You've been spending a lot of time with him lately, haven't you?"

"We've been finishing his house so he could entertain his family from Alabama this weekend."

"How did it look?"

"Really nice. He has a home he can be proud to show off now."

"But you'll still see him, won't you, even though the job is finished? I mean, you and he have obviously been growing closer during the past few weeks."

"Not so close," Rachel muttered. "He didn't let me get close enough to have a chance at making it last with him."

"Oh, dear. Have you two had a quarrel?"

"We broke up—if that's what you could call it, considering there was never anything official between us."

"Oh, I'm sorry, Rachel. I didn't know."

"It's okay," she answered with a shrug. "It just happened today. We both lost our tempers and said some things, and then it escalated and…well, I think it's safe to say it's over between us."

"It happened today? Before or after you rushed off to take care of Robbie and Kaylee?" her mother asked a bit too shrewdly.

"He got mad because Kaylee called me," Rachel conceded. "But you know how I feel about men who get too possessive, Mother. I won't be told when I can help my friends or my family."

"He always complained when you had other obligations?"

"Well, no, not always." He had actually gone with her to help Dani that last time, she thought sadly. "He was usually pretty understanding, or at least I thought so. But today he said some things that really hurt me."

"I'm sorry. But—well, you do spend a lot of time taking care of other people. Myself, included," her mother admitted. "It was always a bone of contention between you and Robbie. And it bothered Rex, too. They sometimes felt like you were pushing them aside. Now, granted, both of them were a bit too smothering for you, but maybe Mark had a legitimate reason to be upset today?"

Remembering his nasty comment about her getting a feeling of superiority out of helping other people, Rachel grew irritated all over again. "I could understand him being annoyed. But it didn't justify the things he said."

"Only you would know that, I suppose. But maybe you should think about everything that was said, just in case there was some validity to some of it."

"I'm sure I will think about it," Rachel muttered. She doubted that she would be able to stop thinking about that fight anytime soon. But she would wait until she was alone to replay it completely in her mind. She wouldn't want to upset her mother by bursting into tears over their tea.

Chapter Fifteen

Mark was up and showered early Sunday morning, trying to be quiet. It felt odd to have other people in his home, but not in a bad way, he decided.

Though there had been a few awkward moments, he'd actually had a fairly nice day with the Brannons yesterday, he mused. Pushing his feelings about the split with Rachel force-fully to the back of his mind, he had concentrated solely on getting to know his family. He thought he'd done a decent job of hiding the fact that she had pretty much kicked him directly in the heart before she'd slipped out of his house, leaving him to make rather lame excuses on her behalf.

The dinner at the Italian restaurant had been particularly nice, even though Mark had been aware of an occasional surreal feeling at being surrounded by so many people who shared his features. He had realized that anyone observing them would see them as a family. He was probably the only one who felt as though he were an imposter among them.

By the time they'd returned to his house, it was late and everyone was tired. He had gone to bed feeling as if he'd gotten to know them fairly well, though he certainly couldn't say he thought of them as parents and brothers just yet. More like a very nice family he wouldn't mind getting to know better. Perhaps the rest would come with time.

He had spent the remainder of the night tossing and turning, unable to avoid for any longer the painful thoughts of Rachel and the hurtful things they had said to each other. Feeling as though he had barely slept a wink, he let the cold shower shock him into semicoherence and then dressed quickly in jeans and a polo shirt and headed downstairs to make breakfast preparations.

Someone had beaten him downstairs.

He stopped short in the kitchen doorway when he saw Elaine at the stove, a wooden spoon in her hand. The welcoming scent of fresh-brewed coffee filled the room and the makings of a hearty breakfast were laid out on the countertop.

"Good morning," she said, giving him a rather misty smile. "I hope you don't mind that I raided your kitchen. I tend to be an early riser, and I love to make breakfast for the family. I wanted to cook for you this morning."

"No, of course I don't mind. Is there anything I can do to help?"

"You can pour yourself a cup of coffee and sit at the bar to talk with me while I cook," she replied. "If I can't find something, you can tell me where it is."

He laughed wryly as he poured coffee into a mug. "You're assuming I would know. We just got the kitchen stocked this past week. I've hardly had time to use anything, myself. But I'm sure together we can find everything."

"Your house really is lovely, Mark. It's a big place for a single man."

"I always wanted a big house I could rattle around in. I grew up in tiny apartments and rent houses. I guess buying a house made me feel like I'd made something of myself."

Her hands faltered for a moment in response to his candid reply, but she continued to make what he assumed were going to be homemade biscuits. "You've definitely done that," she assured him. "I'm so proud of everything you've accomplished."

"Thanks. I hardly remember a time when I didn't want to be a doctor. I guess it was in the genes."

"Maybe it was," she said, turning a quick smile in his direction.

As if in an effort to keep the conversation light, she asked, "Is that fresh parsley I see growing over there?"

"Yes. Rachel planted parsley, rosemary and basil. Snip whatever you need."

"How nice. I like to grow my own herbs at home, too. She really seemed to think of everything, didn't she? Our room was so nice, and we had everything we needed."

"I'm glad you were comfortable."

Sliding the biscuits into the oven, she picked up a package of bacon. "I liked Rachel very much. It was such a shame she had to leave early. You said one of her friends was in trouble?"

"Yeah. She gets called on a lot for that sort of thing."

He had tried not to let resentment tinge his voice, but he might not have been entirely successful. His mother looked at him sharply. "She obviously has a big heart if people feel free to turn to her in times of crisis."

"Yes, well, I think it's become a habit. For everyone else, and for Rachel."

"That happens," Elaine agreed quietly, looking down at the unopened package of bacon. "I got into the habit of volunteering when I was younger. I must have belonged to more than half a dozen organizations. Junior League, PTA, hospital auxiliary, church groups…you name it, I joined it. And once I joined, I couldn't seem to say no to whatever they needed me to do. I ran constantly from one project to another, telling myself that what I was doing was vital to the community. Feeling important because I was making such worthwhile use of my time. The problem was, I was neglecting my own family. Letting other people take on more of the responsibilities in my own home. A housekeeper. A nanny."

She said the last word almost in a whisper. For a moment, Mark was afraid she was going to start crying again, but she cleared her throat and lifted her chin. "I was involved in one of those charitable activities the day you were taken. Helping families who had been displaced by the flood. It was important work, but there were other people who could have taken care of it. People who didn't have three young children at home. Had I stayed at home that day, we never would have lost you. That thought has haunted me every minute of every day for the past thirty years."

"You couldn't have known," he told her gently, realizing that she was trying to apologize to him. "Who could have imagined that she would pull off such a crazy scheme? It was just a series of freak occurrences that made it work, apparently."

"Thank you, dear, but I'll never completely forgive myself. I'm just glad I was given the opportunity to tell you how sorry I am about what happened. How much we all loved you and missed you."

"You don't owe me apologies," he answered gruffly. "I was a toddler. I don't remember any of it. You were the ones who suffered. I can't imagine how much it must have hurt you and, uh—"

"Dad," she supplied quietly. "I hope you'll be able to think of us as Mom and Dad someday."

"I'm trying."

"I know you are, Mark. And we won't pressure you, I promise. I just want you to know that we still love you, very much, and we hope you know we will always be there for you when you need us."

"Thank you. Mom."

She went still for a moment, then set the bacon on the counter and moved toward him. "I'm sorry, but I simply have to hug you. I can't hold back any longer."

He smiled and stood. "I won't try to stop you."

She came barely to his shoulder as she threw her arms around him. He bent his head to gather her closer, and he heard her sniffling into his shoulder as the tears finally escaped. It should have been extremely uncomfortable, but strangely enough, it wasn't so bad.

"Uh-oh. Mom's been set off again." Joel strolled into the room with Nic close behind him. "You must have said something nice, Mark."

"I must have."

His mother dried her eyes and went back to the stove. Mark moved to the table with Joel and Nic. A moment later Lou and Ethan ambled in. "That's a very nice bi-level patio you've got out there, son," Lou approved. "You can have some fine barbecues out there."

"Yes, I plan to have a good grill installed soon. Find some outdoor tables and chairs and stuff to put out by the pool."

"Do you have a good termite plan? With all those trees in your backyard, you'll have to watch for them, you know."

Mark noticed that the others all exchanged amused glances, but he answered seriously, "I have a contract with a company that makes regular inspections, though I haven't lived here long enough for them to come by yet."

"Keep an eye out for them. They can eat an entire house before you know it."

"I'll do that, sir. Uh, Dad. Thanks for the advice."

Lou's face turned a little red, his eyes a bit too bright, but he merely nodded.

Clearing her throat, as if she, too, had been affected by that brief exchange, Nic asked, "Will Rachel be able to join us today, Mark?"

"No, I don't think so."

He was going to leave it at that, but Ethan gave him a hard look. "You two have a spat?"

Family, Mark reminded himself. From what he'd heard, they usually felt quite comfortable asking personal questions. He remembered that spirited dinner with Rachel's family and wondered if he was in for his share of similar experiences in the future, even though the Brannons seemed a bit more reserved than the Madisons overall.

"We, um, had a disagreement," he admitted.

"Nothing serious, I hope," his mother said, sliding a well-filled plate in front of him. "You and Rachel make such a nice couple. I can always tell when my boys are in love."

Both Ethan and Joel gave little snorts of disbelief, which spared Mark the necessity of saying anything, since he wasn't at all sure he could have come up with anything just then.

"Well, I can," Elaine insisted.

"So, how come Mark got served first?" Joel asked, smirking as he made the mock complaint.

"It's his house," she retorted, going back for another plate. "And, besides, he's the baby."

Mark choked as his older brothers grinned mercilessly at him. He could tell he was in for some teasing now.

Oddly enough, he didn't really mind. For one thing, it was better than thinking about what his mother had said about his feelings for Rachel.

Since most of them had jobs to get back to by the next day, the Brannon family left late that afternoon. Their goodbyes were somewhat less awkward than the hellos had been, but no less poignant.

Ethan gripped his hand. "You'll come to the wedding?"

Mark nodded. "I wouldn't miss it."

"I'm holding you to that. Aislinn would be very disappointed if you couldn't make it. And so would I."

"I'll be there."

Nic stood on tiptoes to brush a light kiss against his cheek. "Thanks for being such a great host. We'd love to return the favor at our house in Arkansas. Any time."

He nodded. "That would be nice."

Joel started to take his offered hand, then shook his head and grabbed him in a rough guy-hug. "Welcome back to the family, little brother. We don't want to lose you again."

Returning the hug, Mark replied, "I'm not going anywhere."

He turned to his father. They shook hands, then hugged somewhat clumsily, but no less sincerely. Drawing back, Lou pressed an envelope into Mark's hand.

"What is this?"

"It's a certified copy of your birth certificate. Your legal birth certificate. It lists your name as Kyle Morgan Brannon, of course, but I thought you might like to have it, anyway."

With a lump in his throat, Mark nodded. He would have to decide later how to handle the legalities of his new situation—down to his last name, for that matter. For now, he simply appreciated the gesture.

And then it was time to say goodbye to his mother, at least for the time.

"I'm not going to cry," she promised him, though her eyes were damp. "But it is hard to leave you."

He bent to press a kiss on her soft cheek. "We'll see each other again," he promised. "Soon."

"Bring all the photographs you can find, okay? I want to see what you looked like at every stage of your life."

"I'll try to find them," he promised, having used unpacked boxes in the attic as an excuse not to get them out during this visit. He simply hadn't been ready to look at them yet, and she must have understood, because she hadn't pressed.

She wrapped her arms around him for a long, hard hug, and then forced herself to step back. "Call Rachel, Mark. Whatever you did, tell her you're sorry. This house is too big for you to live in it alone."

A pain shot through his heart, but he managed to keep his smile relatively steady. "What makes you think it was something I did?"

The Brannon men groaned in unison as Nic laughed. "It's always something the guy did, bro," Joel confided. "Might as well get used to it."

"I'll think about it," he told his mother. "Call me to let me know everyone got home all right, will you?"

She beamed. "I would love to."

The lump in his throat was almost painful as he watched them drive away in the car they had rented at the airport. When they were completely out of sight, he moved back into the empty house that Rachel had decorated and closed the door. And then he simply stood there, his back to the door, his eyes closed, an echoing emptiness deep inside his chest.

Rachel stood in front of her open refrigerator Wednesday after work, thinking that it was long past time for a grocery run. She hadn't spent much time at home lately, and her empty shelves were showing it. She closed the door, not really hungry, anyway.

She'd worked at the Perkins house all that day. A number of things had gone wrong, but she'd been able to take care of everything that had popped up. She'd also gotten a lead on a big new contract for which she would be meeting with the potential client on Friday. It would be a challenging, high-profile job that should lead to others like it, just the kind of opportunity she had hoped for since starting her own business.

She was pleased, of course. Thrilled, actually, she assured herself, walking slowly into her living room and sinking onto the couch. Her life was in a good place right now. Her business was doing well. She was paying her bills and able to even put a little away for the future. Her family seemed to be coming out of the difficult phase they'd been going through for the past year. She'd talked to Dani earlier that day, and her sister seemed to be seeing things through a clearer light. All in all, everything was good.

Everything except her heart, of course. That bore a distinct crack that couldn't be easily patched.

She would recover from this love affair gone sour, she assured herself. She had a full life, a good life. It would be nice to have a loving relationship with someone, but not if it meant that she was the one doing all the giving, all the sharing. But she could grant herself permission to be disappointed that it hadn't worked out with Mark. To be hurt that he'd been so willing to let her go.

She was startled when someone knocked on her door. She wasn't expecting anyone. Thinking it might be Dani, who had talked about coming home that afternoon, she moved to answer it, checking the peephole first, just in case.

Her fingers tightened spasmodically on the doorknob when she identified her caller. Moistening her lips, she slowly opened the door. "Mark?"

He stood in the hallway, one hand at the back of his neck, a slightly brooding expression on his face. "Are you busy? Do you have plans for this evening?"

"Not really. I was just going to work on a design presentation."

"Can you come with me? Just for a little while? There's something I need to show you."

She hesitated, but not for very long. There was no way she could resist the appeal in his eyes. "I'll get my purse."

He didn't look particularly surprised that she had agreed, but then he must have known she would, she thought somberly. Hadn't he accused her of being unable to turn down anyone who asked her for anything?

"Are we going to your house?" she asked when they were belted into his car and he drove out of the parking lot. "Did you find something I missed?"

"No. This has nothing to do with your job."

"Oh." She noticed that he turned in the opposite direction from his home. "So, where are we going?"

"I just need to show you something," he repeated.

She nodded and sat back in her seat, trusting that he had a good reason for this outing. Maybe she didn't always know what he was thinking or feeling, might be frustrated by his obtuseness when it came to what she had needed from their relationship, but she did trust him, she realized.

And still she was startled when he drove through the gates of a large cemetery. "Um—Mark?"

"Just wait." He made several turns with the familiarity of someone who had visited this place many times. He parked on the side of the paved road next to a neatly tended section of headstones, many decorated with bright silk flowers in bronze vases.

She climbed out of the car when he did, following him to a headstone set beneath a large, leafy tree. The shade from the tree stretched far across the ground as the sun lowered in the early-evening sky. A small concrete bench had been placed next to the grave, which was marked with a simple but pretty granite headstone. An arrangement of yellow and white silk flowers looked new enough to still be clean and bright.

The name on the marker said Carmen Thomas. According to the dates, she had been in her midfifties when she'd died. A line across the bottom of the stone said simply, Beloved Mother.

Mark sat on the bench, looking somberly at the stone. "I came here pretty often. Just to make sure the flowers looked fresh and the grounds were tended. Sometimes I talked to her, telling her the good things that were happening to me, thinking she would be proud to know that my plans were all working out. I was all she ever had, you know. She told me so all the time. Told me that nothing was more important to her than seeing me happy."

"Oh, Mark," she said, sitting beside him and placing a hand on his knee.

"She was my mother," he said roughly, still focused on that headstone. "At least, I thought she was. I might not have really known her, might never have completely understood her, but I always knew she loved me. And I—"

"You loved her," she finished quietly when his voice faded away.

"She was my mother," he repeated, his voice cracking a little. "How could she…?"

She rested her cheek on his shoulder, pushing her own pain aside for the moment. "I'm so sorry you were hurt this way. I can't imagine how you must be feeling, but I know you did nothing to deserve this."

He reached into his shirt pocket and pulled out a photograph, which he then handed to her. She looked down at it, her throat tightening when she saw the small, smiling boy who had grown into the complex man sitting next to her. The plain, but pleasant-looking woman who sat next to him, pride glowing in her brown eyes.

"I couldn't talk about her. To you. Especially not to the Brannons. It hurt too much. And I knew they would have a hard time understanding the way I felt about her. They're all so angry, so bitter—and they have every right to be. But…"

"But your memories of her were mostly good ones."

He nodded. "Yeah. Mostly."

"You knew I would understand."

"I—yeah. I figured you would."

She lifted her head to study his face. "Then why was it so hard to talk to me?"

"It seemed that everyone in your life wanted something from you. I didn't want to be just one of the walking wounded you had to deal with."

"I never thought of you that way."

"Maybe I thought of myself that way. I'm used to being the doctor," he admitted candidly. "Not the patient."

"You helped me when Dani was in trouble. I wanted to think we were there for each other."

"Maybe it's just hard for me to really trust anyone again right now. I mean, you came into my life at the same time my whole world changed. When everything I thought I knew about my past, my very identity had changed. When I had learned that the one person I'd trusted my entire life lied to me until the day she died."

"And I kept running out on you to take care of other people's problems," she said grimly. "No wonder you weren't sure whether to believe me when I said I was there for you."

"I wasn't using you as a distraction from my problems," he said, reminding her of some of the things they'd said in that bitter quarrel. "I simply wasn't letting myself think about them— whether you were there or not."

They sat for several long minutes looking at the headstone, his hand covering hers on his leg. And then Mark broke the silence. "I'd like to try again, Rachel. I've missed you."

"I've missed you, too," she replied candidly. "But—"

"But I hurt you."

"Yes."

"I'm sorry. I could make a lot of excuses, but the truth is, I was wrong. I had no right to try to stop you from going to a friend who needed you."

She sighed. "But you needed me then, too—despite what you said to the contrary. And you must have felt as if I bailed on you to take care of my ex-husband's hysterical wife. Which I did, of course. I let her manipulate me and I was wrong to leave when I'd told you I'd be there."

"We were both under stress."

Without looking at him, she said, "I can't change who I am, Mark. I can't stop being there for my family and friends, though I will try to be better at setting boundaries and priorities. You were right about that. I do need to make it clear that I have my own life and that they should try to solve some of their problems on their own before calling me."

"Why would I want you to change?" he asked evenly. "I fell in love with you exactly the way you are. Soft heart, generous spirit and all."

Her hand twitched on his leg. His tightened over it. After a long pause, Rachel said, "I fell in love with you, too."

"Past tense?" he asked, his voice very low.

"Past. Present. Future."

He looked at her then, his eyes a bit red-rimmed. "I love you, Rachel."

"I love you, too."

He brushed his lips over hers, little more than a whisper of a kiss, and then stood and held his hand down to her. "Let's go home."

She detained him for a moment when he would have walked away. Standing beside him, looking down at Carmen Thomas's grave, she asked, "Will you come here again?"

His jaw twitched as he followed her gaze. "Do you think I should?"

For some reason, the thought of this grave lying lonely and unvisited in the future made her very sad. "I think you should. Every once in a while, maybe. To remember the things that made you the man you are today."

"Then maybe I will," he said, draping an arm around her shoulders and turning her toward the car. "Someday."

Neither of them looked back as they walked away together.

Epilogue

"These shoes are killing me."

Rachel laughed as Nic Brannon slipped into a folding chair beside hers on the back deck of Ethan's riverside home. "Then why did you wear them?"

Holding one foot out for inspection, Nic replied, "Because they make my legs look so darned good."

Rachel laughed again. "I'll grant you that one. They look great."

Sighing, Nic lowered her foot. "So maybe I can tolerate them for another couple of hours. Monday it's back to the ugly but comfortable work shoes that go with my uniform. So, where's Mark?"

Smiling, Rachel replied, "He had to take a call on his cell. One of his patients had a problem that needed his consultation."

Nic groaned. "Been there, done that. It's a hazard of being with a doctor who tends to get overinvolved with his patients. Joel's phone rings all the time."

"It's the same with Mark. But I can't complain, since when his isn't ringing, mine is."

Wrinkling her nose, Nic nodded. "Mine, too. I guess it's just the joys of modern communications, huh?"

"Must be."

Looking around at the small, but lively crowd around them, Nic commented, "It was a nice wedding, wasn't it? Simple, but elegant. Just like the bride."

Glancing at the lovely flower-decked arbor on the dock on which Aislinn and Ethan had been married less than an hour earlier, Rachel agreed, "It was a beautiful wedding. They both look so happy."

"So does Mark, by the way. Being a Brannon seems to agree with him."

Rachel looked around to find him approaching, his eyes on hers, a smile of rueful apology on his perfect mouth. "Yes, it does."

Nic rose again, groaning lightly when her abused feet took her weight. "Looks like Elaine wants to speak with me. I'll catch you later, Rachel."

"Of course."

A moment later, Mark slid into the chair Nic had vacated. "Sorry. I didn't know the call would take quite that long."

"I'm fine. Did you get it taken care of?"

"Yes, I think so. Can I get you anything else to eat or drink?"

She groaned. "I couldn't eat another bite. They put on quite a spread, didn't they?"

"I've heard rumors that the Brannons love to eat."

She laughed. "Imagine that."

He glanced around as if to make sure they were alone in their cozy corner of the large deck. "I've been doing some thinking, Rachel."

Glancing away from the officious-acting woman who seemed to be trying to organize a line dance on the other end of the deck—Rachel had been told that her name was Heidi and that she was Dr. Lou Brannon's office manager—she looked curiously at Mark. "Thinking about what?"

"Officially changing to my real name. Not the Kyle part, it's too late to start answering to that. But I think I'd like to be known as Mark Brannon from now on. It just seems right, somehow."

The lump that had formed in her throat made her voice a bit shaky. "I think that would make your parents very happy. It would show them that you consider yourself a full member of the family now."

"It's going to be sort of complicated, getting everything changed over and trying to explain to everyone."

"Yes. But you can do it. Women do it all the time," she added with a smile.

"True. And, speaking of that—"

He reached out to take her hand. "Any chance you'd like to be a Brannon, too?"

She blinked. "Are you, um—"

"Proposing?" He grinned. "Maybe I could have picked a better time and place, but, yeah. I guess I am. Will you marry me, Rachel? Will you share a family cell phone plan with me?"

She laughed shakily and leaned over to catch his face in her hands. "We'll discuss the cell phone plan later. But the answer to your question is yes. I would love to marry you. On the condition that you'll let me redecorate occasionally."

"As often as you like," he promised recklessly, then pressed his mouth to hers in a long, hard kiss.

"Mark?" His mother skidded to a stop nearby. "Oh, sorry. I just wondered if you would join us at the trellis. Your uncle is going to take some family pictures."

"Of course." He stood and held out his hand to Rachel. "Just be sure to use my full name on the back of the photographs," he added to his mother. "Dr. Mark Brannon."

Elaine caught her breath as the significance of that statement struck her. "Mark Brannon," she whispered, reaching up to stroke his cheek. "Such a nice name."

Kissing his mother's hand, he kept it in his as he said, "Rachel thinks so, too. In fact, she's just agreed to become a Brannon, herself."

Elaine kissed both of Rachel's cheeks in delight. "I'm so happy for you both. For all of us. We've gotten our son back, and now we're getting a new daughter."

"Mark should have waited to tell you later," Rachel fretted, glancing at the group gathering on the dock. "This is Ethan and Aislinn's day."

Elaine laughed and stood between them, tucking their arms into hers as she led them off the deck. "Trust me, dear, they'll be delighted to share this good news. This family has learned never to waste a chance to celebrate the happy times we can spend with each other."

Smiling at Mark over his mother's head, Rachel decided that would be the motto for the new life she and Mark were about to begin together.

* * * * *

*Mills & Boon® Special Edition
brings you a sneak preview of Christine Rimmer's*
In Bed with the Boss,
which is available in May 2009.

*Little did hotel-chain CFO Tom Holloway realise
that his new executive assistant spelled trouble.
But even though single mum Shelly Winston was
planted by Holloway's worst enemy to take him
down, Shelly was no fool – she had a mind of her
own and an eye for her handsome boss!*

*Don't miss this exciting new story coming next
month from Mills & Boon® Special Edition!*

In Bed with the Boss

by

Christine Rimmer

Two years ago…

It was *the* moment.

And Tom Holloway knew it.

Across the black granite boardroom table, Helen Taka-Hanson waited, her beautiful face composed, showing him nothing. Behind her, beyond the floor-to-ceiling windows, the afternoon sun reflected off the tall buildings of North Michigan Avenue. Tom kept his gaze level, on Helen. But he knew what was out there: The Second City. The Magnificent Mile.

Chicago. Tom wanted it. *Needed* it, really. A fresh start in a new town. He would be chief financial officer of TAKA-Hanson's new hospitality division.

Which meant hotels. Contemporary luxury hotels on a grand scale. It was the biggest venture he'd tackled so far and it sounded good. Better than good.

And the job was his. Helen had already made the offer.

What he said next could blow it for him—more than likely *would* blow it for him. Which was why he'd left the crucial information off his résumé. His disgrace had happened so long ago, it was easily glossed over now.

But Tom had learned the hard way that concealment didn't work in the long term. The high-stakes world of finance was too damn small. In the end, his past always found him.

Better to show his stuff first, let them know he had the chops, get all the way to the job offer. And then take a deep breath and lay the bad news right out there.

The offer just might stand in spite of his past. If it didn't, if he lost the job, well, chances were he would have lost it anyway in the end, when the ugly facts surfaced.

Oh, yeah. A delicate moment, this. The moment of truth.

Helen said, "Well, Tom. You've heard our offer. Is there anything else we need to go over?"

Tom sat back in the chair, ordered his body to relax and told himself—for the hundredth time—that it had to be done.

"As a matter of fact, Helen. There is something else…"

She arched a brow at him and waited for him to go on.

He said, "I was fired once. It was a long time ago, my first job out of Princeton."

"Fired." Helen spoke the word flatly. "That's not on your résumé, is it?"

"No. And it gets worse."

"I'm listening."

"I was young and way too hungry, working on Wall Street, determined to make it big and do it fast. None of which is any justification for my actions. I was discharged for insider trading. And then I was arrested for it. And convicted. I did six months."

A silence. A pretty long one. Tom could feel yet another great job slipping away from him.

At last, Helen asked the big question. "Were you guilty?"

"Yes. I was."

He might have softened the harsh fact a little. He could have explained what a naive idiot he'd been then. He could have told her all about his mentor at the time, who'd convinced him to pass certain "tips" to big clients. He could have said that the guy got away clean by setting Tom up to take the fall for him. That the same former mentor had been a curse on his life since then. Because of that one man, Tom had lost out on a number of opportunities—and not just in terms of his career. It would have been the truth.

However, his former boss wasn't the one up for CFO, TAKA-Hanson, hospitality division. Tom was. His prospective employer needed to know that he'd once broken the law—and then gone to jail for it. The why and the wherefore?

Not the question.

Tom sat unflinching, waiting for the ax to fall.

Instead, Helen smiled.

It was a slow smile, and absolutely genuine—a warm smile, the kind of smile that would make any red-blooded man sit up and take notice. From what Tom had heard, this genius of the business world, now in her late forties, had saved Hanson Media from collapse several years back, after her first husband, George Hanson, died suddenly. The story went that before she was forced to step in and save the family business, she'd been a trophy wife.

Smart and savvy and strictly professional as she'd been since he met her, Tom had been having trouble seeing her as mere arm candy for a tycoon. But now he'd been granted that amazing smile, he wasn't having trouble anymore.

That face, that smile…

George Hanson had been one lucky man. And so was her current husband, TAKA-Hanson's chairman of the board, Morito Taka.

"I prize honesty," Helen said. "I prize it highly. So I think it's time I repaid your truth with one of my own. I've done my homework on you, Tom. I've known all along about how you lost that trading job, and the price you paid for what you did. I've been interested to see if you'd tell me about it. And now that you have, I'm more certain than ever on this. Other than that one admittedly serious black mark against you—for which you've paid your dues—your record is spotless. I know you'll make a fine addition to my team. I've got no res-ervations. You're the man for this job."

Tom's heart slammed against his breastbone. Had he

heard right? Had it worked out, after all? The CEO knew the truth.

And she'd hired him anyway.

He held out his hand. Helen took it. They shook.

When he spoke, his voice was firm and level. "I intend to make sure you never regret this decision."

"I believe you," said Helen. "That's another reason you're our new CFO."

His passions were as tempestuous as his temper...

Even though Kate Whittman was young and inexperienced, she wanted moody Texas rancher Jason Donovan more than anything. But he offered her only brotherly protection.

So Kate pursued another fantasy – becoming a successful New York fashion designer. But just when it seemed that her fairy tale was coming true, fate brought her back to Texas. And to Jason.

Available 1st May 2009

www.millsandboon.co.uk   M&B

2 FREE

BOOKS AND A SURPRISE GIFT!

We would like to take this opportunity to thank you for reading this Mills & Boon® book by offering you the chance to take TWO more specially selected titles from the Special Edition series absolutely FREE! We're also making this offer to introduce you to the benefits of the Mills & Boon® Book Club™—

- ★ FREE home delivery
- ★ FREE gifts and competitions
- ★ FREE monthly Newsletter
- ★ Exclusive Mills & Boon Book Club offers
- ★ Books available before they're in the shops

Accepting these FREE books and gift places you under no obligation to buy, you may cancel at any time, even after receiving your free shipment. Simply complete your details below and return the entire page to the address below. You don't even need a stamp!

YES! Please send me 2 free Special Edition books and a surprise gift. I understand that unless you hear from me, I will receive 4 superb new titles every month for just £3.19 each, postage and packing free. I am under no obligation to purchase any books and may cancel my subscription at any time. The free books and gift will be mine to keep in any case.

E9ZED

Ms/Mrs/Miss/Mr ....Initials ....
BLOCK CAPITALS PLEASE

Surname ....

Address ....

....

....Postcode............................

Send this whole page to:
UK: FREEPOST CN81, Croydon, CR9 3WZ